RAVISHED

CATHERINE ALBA

HEATHER

LESS THAN HALF AN HOUR AFTER leaving Florence, I was convinced that I wasn't going to survive this car journey. I just didn't know what was going to kill me first. The suffocating heat that was making my entire body sticky and itchy? Or the frantic Italian drivers that didn't seem to care a delicious fig about lanes, speed limits, indicators, or blind spots?

The Autostrada had four lanes in both directions, and all eight lanes were packed with huge thundering lorries that were hurling along way over the speed limit. A million little Fiats and Seats were buzzing all around my equally minute rental car like a swarm of flies. Since I hadn't been able to figure out the display that controlled the air conditioning unit, I had rolled down the window, and the stench of exhaust fumes and the noise from the surrounding traffic was overwhelming all my senses. The sweat trickled from underneath my breasts down over my belly and the only good thing about this day was that there was no one else in the car to see me in this state.

Why, oh, why had I decided that an excursion into the Tuscan countryside would be a good idea on a scorching hot day like this? And why had I insisted on going alone? Everyone I had spoken to in Florence had told me to stay in the city, or to take the train if I wanted to explore more of Italy. They had warned me about Italian drivers and their fatalistic approach to road safety. Had I listened? Of course not.

Yep. I was going to die here. And it would be my own fault.

My grip on the steering wheel hardened when I suddenly saw five of the small Italian cars line up, side by side, in front of me. Sure, there were only four lanes, but hey, their cars were small enough to fit half-a-dozen across the Autostrada, so why not?

Because that is not how you do things! a part of my brain wanted to scream. Checking all the mirrors, I squeezed into the lorry lane on the far right. It was cramped and the tall lorry in front of me meant that I couldn't see anything at all up ahead, but my exit had to be coming up soon and I didn't want to wait until the last minute.

I debated getting off the Autostrada early, just to get away from this madness, but I didn't want to waste all of this lovely sunlight driving. Smaller roads would probably be less frantic than this, but it would take me that much longer to reach my destination, so I was determined to tough it out. I could do this! Surely it couldn't be much further.

At that exact moment, my phone chirped into life on the passenger seat. The car had a built-in GPS, of course, but it only spoke Italian, and had been as uncooperative as the A/C. "At the next exit, turn right," my phone said. I breathed a sigh of relief and flicked on my indicator signal. Finally!

Leaving the Autostrada wasn't as big of a

relief as I had expected, though. The traffic turned out to be almost as intense on the smaller country roads, and there were a lot more distractions to take into consideration. I bit my lip and leaned forward, peering at the signs at a crossroads. My phone had told me to take a right turn, but the signs seemed to indicate that I should continue straight ahead.

I decided to obey my phone and hoped it wouldn't lead me too far astray.

It wasn't until I had taken a couple more turns onto incrementally smaller and smaller roads that I found myself alone on the road and could finally begin to calm down. The inside of the car was still sweltering, but the open window let me experience all the enticing scents of the Tuscan countryside. It was intoxicating and I stopped regretting going on this adventure. This was going to be a great day. I would get to see so much that I would never have experienced in Florence. The stories I would have to tell!

It was a pity that the road was so winding and unpredictable because that meant that I couldn't see much of the scenic surroundings. The small glimpses I got here and there made my fingers itch to pull out my paints. Everywhere I looked, there was something that I desperately wanted to capture on canvas. Tall pointy cypress trees standing in attention down a ruler-straight side road. A picturesque farmyard with lush flower boxes decorating the dilapidated house, chickens wandering casually around the front yard. A single pair of trousers on a clothesline. The round, rolling hills stretching into eternity in varying shades of greens and blues under the crisp morning sky. An ancient village on a hilltop almost gleaming with a dull orange terracotta sheen in the sun, looking exactly as it must have done 500 years ago, as if I had driven through a portal when I exited the Autostrada and traveled back to the renaissance.

"At the next turning, turn right," my phone said, bringing me back to the 21st century, and I sat up and started scanning the road ahead for an exit. I couldn't see any side road, but there was a sharp curve up ahead that blocked my view. The exit must be right around the corner.

I had slowed down significantly by the time I came round the bend, and that was fortunate because right in the middle of the road, just in front of the exit, was an animal. A large and rather dirty goat, chewing slowly and regarding the approaching car with complete indifference. I slammed my foot on the brake and one hand on the horn before swerving over in the opposite lane without even having time to check the mirrors. Fortunately, I was alone on the road and I avoided being crushed into a pulp by an Italian lorry.

*Un*fortunately, the goat was startled by the sound of the horn and bounced away across the gravelly tarmac, straight into the path of the skidding little Fiat. I turned the wheel again, trying desperately to avoid hitting the panicked goat, and with my heart in my throat I felt the tires lose their grip on the gravel-covered tarmac. The back end of the small rental started to slide toward the edge of the road, and I panicked. Twisting the wheel back and forth and stepping hard on the brake did not make the small car stop. Instead, it started to spin around, while still sliding toward the opposite side of the road.

"At first opportunity, make a U-turn, and then turn right," my phone said, but I didn't know which way was right anymore. Everything was spinning; my head, the car, the surrounding trees.

And then one of the back tires slipped off the edge of the tarmac, and the small car tipped off the road and down a steep slope. I screamed, but if there was anyone around who heard me—apart from the traffic-obstructing goat—I didn't see them. All I could see through the windscreen was the clear blue Tuscan sky. The engine whirred and branches snapped and cracked when the car rolled backward through some bushes and then finally slowed down as the ground leveled out, coming to a stop with a low thud.

I stared at my hands gripping the steering wheel as I listened to the ticking noise from the car's engine and the whooshing sound that was the blood pulsing in my eardrums. My heart was racing, but as it slowly dawned on me that I was unharmed, and that the car had stopped its wild careening down the slope, it started to slow down. I took a deep breath and loosened my grip on the wheel. My fingers felt stiff and cold, despite the heat. After the intense noise that had surrounded me just a moment ago, the silence down here was deafening.

I switched off the engine and looked around. The car had plowed backward down a steep slope covered in brambles and bushes. I could see the path it had taken. Somewhere up there was the road. I turned in my seat and looked behind the car. There was a field. Some cows were standing under a tree in the middle of the field, looking at me with obvious disinterest in their eyes. The car had been stopped by the fence surrounding their field, a rusty barbed-wire affair that looked like it had been there for a hundred years or more. The brambles and bushes must have slowed the car down because that fence would never have withstood an out-of-control car. Not even this tiny Fiat.

Rubbing my face with trembling hands, I took stock. I was fine. The car was fine. The goat hadn't been hurt. The cows were fine. Everyone and everything was fine.

Apart from the fact that the car wasn't on the road, where it was supposed to be. It was nowhere near the road, and I was not going to be able to drive up that steep slope, not in this car.

Pushing my seat back, I undid the seatbelt and reached for the water bottle in the tote that was standing in the foot well on the passenger side. The water was tepid but tasted like nectar after the long thirsty drive. I made another attempt at switching on the A/C, but the small screen just kept spouting Italian error messages in red boxes, and I didn't dare click on any of the alternatives, in case it caused the car to self-destruct.

I took another sip of the lukewarm water and looked around.

Now, what was I going to do?

The obvious answer was to call for help, but call who? I didn't know where I was, and I didn't know who could help me out of this situation. Did they have AA in Italy? And if so, would my travel insurance cover the expense of getting the car towed?

The only phone number I had added to my phone book before setting off was that of the emergency services, but … this didn't really qualify as an emergency, in my eyes. I wasn't hurt. The car might have been damaged somehow by going through those bushes, but this wasn't exactly a car *crash*, now was it? I didn't need an ambulance, or angry Italian policemen breathalyzing me and throwing me in an Italian jail for endangering the local livestock.

No, what I needed was a tow truck. Or perhaps just a farmer with a tractor or something that could pull me back up onto the road.

I glanced in the rear-view mirror at the cows that were still lounging in the shade underneath the tree. Where there were cows, there must be a farmer. All I had to do was find the farm.

I gathered my things from the console and stuffed my phone and water bottle in the tote. Then I pushed open the door and turned in my seat, but then I froze and just stared at the ground outside.

The car was surrounded by lush greenery on all sides. I had been aware of that. What I *hadn't* noticed until just now was that the greenery in question consisted of nettles.

Tall, lush stinging nettles that grew in a wide field all along the outside of the fence.

I was suddenly very much aware of the fact that my legs were bare underneath my long, flowy skirt, and that my sandals were strappy and offered no protection whatsoever to the burning sensation of nettles.

I craned my neck and looked out the window on the passenger side, but the field of nettles continued over on that side as well, for as far as I could see.

I was trapped.

Now what?

Turning in my seat I looked up and down the field. There was no house in sight, no road, no sign of life, apart from the cows.

"How about a little help, guys?" I said, but they didn't respond. Just stared at me while their lower jaws ground away at whatever they were masticating. Grass, presumably.

I sank back against the seat with a sigh. A low engine sound passed by somewhere up there, where the road must be. A passing car. I pressed on the horn, as hard as I could, for as long as I could stand it. When I let go, the engine sound had quietened.

Careful to avoid the nettles, I leaned out of the open door. "Hello!" I shouted. "I'm down here!" Then I listened. Nothing. "Can anyone hear me?" I yelled. Still nothing.

Leaning back against the backrest, I took stock. I was fine, but I couldn't stay here. What if no one came along, ever? Judging by the sound of passing cars, there weren't any signs of what had happened up there on the road. What was I going to do? Stay here until winter, when the nettles presumably withered down?

Rummaging through the tote, I found a single power bar and half a packet of chewing gum. That wasn't going to last me until winter. I had to find a way out of here. Maybe I could climb through the back of the car and try and get out through the trunk? Glancing over my shoulder, I hesitated. It was a tiny car, with an even tinier trunk. And I was a big girl. A big and not particularly flexible woman in my prime. No, climbing out through the trunk was not an option. I might not even be able to open the trunk with the fence in the way. No, that would have to be a last resort.

At least the car was in the shade, and I had some water. I would be fine.

Someone would come along.

Everything was going to be just fine.

2

MARCO

I WAS LOST in my thoughts and moving on autopilot when I spotted the car. I stopped and stared at it. A car, right in the middle of my best nettle plot. How on earth …?

Looking up the slope, I could see the path of destruction.

Damn.

People were always driving too fast around here, even on these narrow roads. They only had themselves to blame. Not that I cared.

As long as they didn't destroy my nettles.

I hung the large bucket I had brought with me on one of the fence posts and pulled on my gardening gloves. Then I started harvesting. The nettles were at their peak right now. In a week or so, they would start to go rough and the taste would change. This would be the last week this year that I would make my famous nettle soup. I would have to think of something else for next week.

The car was right in the middle of the patch, and I wasn't planning on harvesting enough that I'd have to go near it, but I decided to check that the fence hadn't been damaged. I didn't want the cows to get out.

Pushing my way through the thick vegetation, I leaned over to see the back of the car. It was pressing up against the fence but didn't seem to have broken anything. There wasn't even any damage on the car, despite the rough path it had cut through the vegetation. When I stood up, I noticed that the door on the driver's side was open. That was strange. I peered inside and was startled to see that there was someone in there. Moving up along the passenger side of the car, I saw a lifeless woman in the driver's seat. My annoyance was immediately replaced by an ice-cold fear. Was she dead?

The chill in my chest made my entire

body freeze and I just stood there, staring at her, for what felt like an eternity. I had to do something, but I couldn't make myself step any closer. Couldn't make myself touch her. My fingers already knew what her dead skin would feel like. Cold. Unnatural. I knew but didn't want to know. Didn't ever want to experience that horror again.

Because of the tall trees casting their shade in this direction, it was dark inside the car, but I could see her clearly. She was beautiful. Serene. At peace.

There was nothing horrifying about the sight of her. No blood anywhere. No sign of trauma. She was leaned against the backrest, her head slumped to one side so that her face turned slightly toward me. Her long, chestnut hair framed a young and beautiful face, and the deep red color of her lips was a powerful contrast to her soft, pale cheeks. I had seen death, and *that* was not what it looked like.

Moving closer to the car, I raised one hand and tapped gently on the window.

The woman startled and her eyes flew open, staring straight at me. Despite the dark hair, her eyes were a bright and unexpected blue, and the intensely red lips parted in a surprised gasp.

"Are you all right?" I asked.

She just stared at me.

"*Signorina*? Do you need help? Shall I call an ambulance?"

As soon as I had said the words, I realized that I didn't have my phone on me. It was probably lying on my desk somewhere, buried in papers. *Those aren't papers; they are overdue bills*, the nasty voice at the back of my head chimed in, but I ignored it.

She still didn't reply, just stared at me. Then something seemed to trigger her into action, and she leaned over and opened the passenger door.

"Hi!" she said, and my eyebrows rose toward my hairline. An American? "I must have dozed off. It sure is hot today!" She fanned herself with one hand and glanced over her shoulder at the cows in the field. "Are those your cows?" She pointed toward the back of her car. "Is that your fence? Did I break it? I'm so sorry. I didn't mean to. It's just—"

"Are you hurt?" I asked, switching to English.

She shook her head. "No, just a bit freaked out." Glancing down at my gloved hands, she continued, "Could you help me get out of here, do you think?"

I didn't understand. If she wasn't hurt, what was she doing, just sitting here? "Do you need an ambulance," I repeated, in English this time.

She smiled, and the smile made her already beautiful face light up from inside in a way that disturbed me. Made me angry. Made me regret having come here. Why couldn't I have decided on another *antipasto* for this evening? It was too late in the season for nettles anyway. What had I been thinking?

"I just need a tow truck," she said. Then she bit her lip. "Unless you've got a tractor."

I stared at her, uncomprehending. "Why would I have a tractor?"

She looked back at me, looking as confused as I felt. "Aren't you the farmer?"

I shook my head. "No, I'm not." I put one hand on the passenger door and leaned forward, peering into the small car. "If you can walk, then what are you—"

My voice broke off mid-sentence when my eyes fell on her bare legs under the steering wheel. The heat in the car had made her hitch up her long skirt all the way to the top of her thighs and the smooth-as-velvet skin reminded me of peaches in cream. I forced my eyes away from the glorious sight and looked around the car. My delicious nettles, everywhere.

"Yeah," she said. "Those darn weeds are all over, and I'm in sandals." She looked at my gloved hand, resting on top of the passenger door. "Could you clear a path for me, do you think? And maybe help me call for assistance, since you speak the lingo?"

I looked inside the car again. "You haven't called for a tow truck?"

She shook her head. "I didn't know who to call."

I frowned. "And how long have you been sitting here?"

She glanced at the clock on the dashboard and seemed startled at what she saw. "Two hours," she said with a slight panic and a lot of annoyance. "I must have dozed off. Damn it."

I took a step back and beckoned to her to come over to the passenger side. "Come here. I will carry you through the nettles."

Her eyes widened and her cheeks turned a bright red. "Oh no," she said firmly. "That's *not* gonna happen." She gestured at the nettles. "Can't you just pull them out to make a path for me. You're wearing gloves."

I frowned. "No, I don't need that many."

It was clear from her face that she didn't understand. "Well, you won't be able to carry me," she said, looking me up and down. "No offense and all that, but you don't exactly look like the Hulk from where I'm sitting."

I wasn't sure what she meant by that. "Move over here," I said, gesturing to the passenger seat. "I will carry you."

She looked like she was going to protest again, but instead, she did as I had said. She had to lift her legs high to get across the mid console, and I was offered an even more generous vista of those glorious thighs before she slid into the passenger seat and pulled her skirt down. I leaned forward and slid one arm under her legs and the other around her back.

"I'm telling you right now, you're not going to be able to—" she said but stopped talking abruptly as I picked her up and started walking back toward the edge of the nettle patch.

I was grateful for the thick gloves, so that I didn't have to feel her warm skin with my bare hands. It was bad enough that I had her soft, round body pressing up against my chest, and her light and delicate scent invaded my nostrils with every breath. I pushed through the nettles over to the edge of the patch and put her down on the path I had made through the tall grass, coming here almost every day for the last couple of months. Then I quickly took a step back to get away from her alluring body. There was a part of me that hadn't wanted to let go of her, and I couldn't let that part get the upper hand. Never again. Oh no.

"I will lock the car," I said. "Is there anything in there that you need? The tow truck might be a while."

"My tote bag," she said, and I turned and

waded back through the greenery, making sure to take the same way, so as not to crush any more of the delicious nettles than was absolutely necessary. Leaning inside the car to retrieve the tote bag and the key fob, I heard her calling out behind me. "And my paints. They're in the backseat."

Glancing over the backrest, I spotted a large wooden box with a handle. I had to open the back door to get it out. When all the car doors were closed and locked, I made my way back to her. She reached for her things, but I only handed her the tote and the key fob. The wooden box was heavy, and it was a bit of a walk back. I retrieved my bucket of nettles from the fence post and gestured at her to walk ahead of me. The path wasn't wide enough for us to walk side by side.

Walking behind her didn't however offer me the relief that I had hoped for. Sure, I didn't have to see her beautiful face, but the sight of her round hips moving back and forth, causing the thin skirt to sway from side to side, was enough to make my chest constrict. And those round buttocks, clearly visible through the thin fabric with no panty line in sight. Wasn't she wearing any underwear? I tightened my grip on the heavy wooden box and forced myself to look away.

We reached the end of the path, at the edge of the field. A wooden door was partially hidden by the ivy that enveloped most of the stone wall that surrounded the property.

"Through here," I said, leaning past her to open the door. It was warped from age and often stuck against the door frame unless you gave it a hard tug.

Her eyes widened when the door flung open. She glanced at me, as if to try and decide if she should go with me. Then she peered inside suspiciously.

What she saw on the other side of the door made her suspiciousness vanish, though, and she gave off a small gasp. "Oh my …"

"Please, enter," I said. "I will call the garage. You can wait here until all the arrangements are made."

She stepped through the door, looking around her. "What is this place?" she said, breathlessly.

"This is the *Monasterio de Camillo*."

Her head spun round, and she stared at me. "A monastery? Are you a monk?"

It was probably intended as a joke, but I didn't smile. "It *used to be* a monastery," I said, walking past her toward the kitchen entrance. "Now it is an *Agriturismo*."

"What is that?" she asked, following me on the curved path through the well-kept garden. I didn't notice it anymore, but all the guests seemed very impressed by it. For me, it was just the place where I lived and worked.

"An *Agriturismo* … it's like a hotel in the countryside, where the guests can experience the genuine Italian way of life," I said automatically. I had repeated those words more times than I cared to remember. Apparently, it was not a concept well known outside of Italy.

I opened the kitchen entrance and beckoned her inside. She walked past me without hesitation this time, and up the two small stone steps to the door, disappearing inside.

The kitchen felt dark after the intense sunshine outside, but my eyes soon adjusted, and I walked over to the large kitchen island in the middle of the room and put the bucket of nettles next to the sink. Then I continued through the spacious kitchen, over to my office. She lagged behind and I glanced at her. She was taking it all in with wide eyes, and I tried to picture what it must look like to her. It was a working kitchen with everything that a modern hotel needed, with plenty of sinks, gas burners, ovens, pots and pans, and every utensil known to man arranged neatly above every workstation. It probably looked completely normal for someone coming in from outside, but if she had seen the rest of the building, she would have thought it stood out like a sore thumb, just like I did. But the authorities had their rules, and if I wanted to keep cooking for the guests here, I had to follow them.

Rummaging through the piles of correspondence on my desk, I unearthed my phone, and was relieved to see that there was still some power left in the battery. Scrolling through my contacts, I found the number of the local garage and pressed the little icon.

The phone rang, signal after signal, and I

was just about to hang up when Giacomo picked up.

"Si?"

"Giacomo! It's Marco. There has been an accident. A car went off the road just east of here. Can you come and get it?"

There was no reply at first, and I became aware of the traffic noises in the background. Voices shouting and the roar of lorries going past. "Marco? Is that you?" Giacomo shouted. "I can barely hear you."

"Where are you?"

"There was a pile-up on the Autostrada. They have called in everyone in the district. I'll be here all afternoon." There was a pause. "And I've gotten three other calls while I've been here. I don't know when I can get to your car, I'm afraid. Is it off the road, completely? It's not blocking traffic?"

I turned around and leaned my bottom against the desk. "No, it's far from the road. It's not blocking anything. It's in the middle of my nettle patch."

"Oh no!" I couldn't help but smile at the genuine despair in Giacomo's voice. "But ... your soup?"

"Don't worry," I said reassuringly. "It's nearly the end of the season anyway."

Giacomo muttered something that got lost in the engine noise from another lorry. "I'll come round and get that car out of your nettles tomorrow," he promised.

"Great. And bring Lucia over for dinner one night when you're not working."

"I will!"

I ended the call and put the phone back down. When I returned to the kitchen, the woman was still standing where I had left her, looking interestedly at everything around her.

"I'm sorry," I said. "But there's been a pile-up on the Autostrada, and the man from the garage can't get here today."

A small frown appeared between her eyebrows. "Well, can't you call someone else?"

I shrugged. "There is no one else. Every tow truck in the district is busy."

"But … How do I get my car back on the road?"

"You don't. You will have to make other arrangements. Where were you headed?"

"Siena."

"Well, that's not far. I can call you a taxi. Or, if you have hotel reservations, they might be able to come and pick you up."

"No, I'm staying in Florence." She looked bewildered. "I was just going to Siena on a day trip, to paint. It's supposed to be so beautiful there." She glanced at the window that was mounted high on the wall. "But even if I could get there, I will have missed most of the daylight by now."

"I can find out when there's a train back to Firenze," I said. "And there might be someone here that can take you to the station." I gestured at her to follow. "Come with me."

3

HEATHER

WHAT WAS THIS PLACE?

My eyes couldn't seem to take it all in as I followed the man from the completely modern and functional kitchen and out into a corridor that looked like something medieval. Every room I passed with an open door had large murals, flaking off the tall walls. And nothing tacky or amateurish either. These were impressive works of art, made by a real artist—or several—more than a century ago.

I had never seen anything like it, outside of a museum.

At the end of the corridor, we came to what looked like a reception area. A woman was standing behind a counter, talking on the phone. When the man walked up to her, she held up one finger with a frighteningly long dark-red fingernail to signal that he needed to wait while she ended the call. She put down the phone and smiled at the man that started speaking to her in Italian.

I had no idea what they were saying, but I loved the way it sounded. Especially his voice. It sounded completely different from when he spoke to me in English. His voice was nice then too, of course. Dark and low and authoritative. But when he spoke Italian, it had a completely different melody, and I could feel it all over my body.

A couple came in and walked over to the counter. The woman picked up a key from a hook on the wall behind her and handed it to them, almost without taking her eyes off the man who had saved me from the nettles.

And all of a sudden, the pieces fell into place. This was a hotel. An Agri-whatever he had called it. And it might not be Siena, but it was beautiful, and there must be plenty of motifs around here that I could paint. And if there wasn't, I could always just study the wonderful murals.

The man had stopped talking and turned toward me. "There is a man that can take you to the afternoon train," he said. "But he is away on another errand right now. You will have to wait here a couple of hours. Don't worry. We will take care of everything. Just let us know what you need. Are you hungry? Thirsty? Do you need to call someone?"

"Actually …" I said, glancing at the wall of keys behind the reception desk. "I was wondering if you might have a room for me."

He looked confused. "You don't want to go back to Firenze?"

I shrugged. "I'm in no hurry, actually. I came to Italy to paint, and this is exactly the kind of place I've been looking for. If there is a room available, I will have some time to paint today and tomorrow, while I wait for the car."

The man turned toward the woman again, launching into another Italian melody. The woman smiled and picked a key from the edge of the board. It was different from the others, I noticed, with a larger wooden marker for the room number instead of the brass ones on all the others, and I wondered why.

"Come," the man said, taking the key from the receptionist.

I followed him back through the corridor to the kitchen. There, the man picked up my box of paints and continued out the door where we had come in.

Again, we crossed through the unreal garden and I once again breathed in the scents from the lemon trees and the lavender. A large shrubbery of rosemary right by the path emanated a heavy scent that made me aware of how long it had been since breakfast.

We took another path than the one we'd come in and ended up at a lower wall at the bottom of the garden. When I came closer, I gasped. I had thought that the monastery was on flat ground, but on this side, it seemed that we were on an elevation. On the other side of the low wall, the ground fell away into a long, deep valley with just the sort of beautiful vista that I had glimpsed here and there from the car on the winding roads. Tiny farmhouses dotted the landscape, and on a smaller hill a little further up on my left, one of those picturesque small towns sat basking in the midday sun.

Well, I had found my motif.

This was perfect. I could set up my easel over there and—

The man cleared his throat, and I was pulled back to the present. He had kept walking and was standing in an archway at the end of the path, almost not visible in the shadows.

I hurried after him, hoisting my tote bag up on my shoulder. Why was he taking me away from the building, though? Surely, the hotel rooms were in the building we'd just come from.

But the man disappeared into the darkness and I followed, without fear this time. Whomever this man was, he was no threat, and I was immensely relieved that he had come to my rescue.

On the other side of the archway, we stepped out into the sunlight. On my left was a door and the man was standing by it, fitting the room key into the lock. The sun was directly above us now, and from the grass that edged the path came the sound of cicadas. A climbing plant that covered most of the wall gave off an almost soporific scent. I couldn't even take it all in. Italy was so … overwhelming.

I followed the man in through the door. It was dark inside and before my eyes could adjust, I walked straight into him, where he had stopped right inside the door.

"Oh, pardon me," I blurted out, taking a step back.

He also moved away from the point of impact, so that we ended up standing as far away from each other as the small room allowed. I tried not to blush, but as usual, my cheeks had other plans. I didn't have time to wallow in her embarrassment, though, because I realized that I wasn't standing in a hotel room.

"But …" I said.

It was a small open-space living area, with a kitchen on one side and a seating area on the other. A door leading off to my right revealed the corner of a desk and a matching chair. The man gestured me toward the door. I walked over to it.

The desk was standing under the window in a bedroom, with a large double bed made of dark wood, stunning against the white-washed walls. The only other piece of furniture was a huge wardrobe over in the corner. It was made out of the same dark wood as the desk and the bed and looked as if it contained a portal into another world. Next to the wardrobe was another door, standing ajar, revealing an en suite bathroom.

"OK …" I said, taking it all in. "Not quite what I had expected, but …"

"You don't like it?" he asked. "You can have another room. A regular hotel room. I just thought you would appreciate the privacy, and the extra space."

My cheeks blossomed again. Was that an insult? I pulled myself tall and wished that I didn't feel so sticky and smelly after my hours in the hot car. It wasn't easy to keep up my usual goddess vibe when I felt like something that had crawled out of the drains. I desperately needed a shower.

"I …" I began, but words failed me.

"For your paints," he continued, holding up my box. My heavy painter's suitcase that he had lugged all this way. "I thought you might need the extra space for your paints."

Once again, glowing cheeks. There was something going on here, something more than a language barrier. I needed to get a grip.

Pushing a smile onto my weary lips, I took a step toward him, relieving him of the heavy wooden box.

"You have been an absolute life saver," I said. "And I don't even know your name."

He didn't smile back. That threw me for a bit. Men usually did. "Marco," he said and proffered his hand.

"Pleased to meet you, Marco. I'm Heather." I shook his hand and was surprised by how smooth it was. I had expected callouses, for some reason. If he spent part of his workday clearing weeds, he must be some kind of handyman around here. A caretaker.

I carried my painter's box out into the living area and set it down on the table. Opening the lid, I let my hand slide over all the little tubes of paint. It reassured me, as it always did. Enough to turn toward him—Marco—with renewed confidence.

"Well, Marco. I can't thank you enough."

He walked toward the door. "It is almost lunch time," he said. "If you have been in that car all morning, you must be hungry. We don't serve lunch here, but if you come into the kitchen, you can get something to eat."

I gestured to the small kitchenette. "That won't be necessary. It looks like I've got everything I need here," I said. "Is there a supermarket nearby? So that I can stock up?"

Marco shook his head. "No. You will need a car to go to the supermarket. But just come into the kitchen; I will make sure that you don't starve. Dinner is not until 8."

And just like that, he left. I stood there for a long time, just staring at the closed door. What a strange man. He spoke very good English for a handyman. Most of the people I had met during my first weeks in Italy had spoken English, but they lived in Florence and met tourists all the time. Several people had warned me that I couldn't expect the Italians out in the countryside to understand what I said. I should have learned the language before coming here.

Well, languages weren't where my talents lay. With one last check of the contents of my painter's box, I grabbed my tote bag and went into the bathroom. I wished that I had a change of clothes, but I hadn't planned to be away overnight. Emptying the sizable tote, I surveyed my resources.

I had brought some makeup for freshening up. My bathing suit, in case I'd found a beach or a pool. A sarong to cover up what the bathing suit didn't conceal. A cardigan, in case the night got chilly. Well now, that was practically a complete outfit!

Peeling off the sweaty blouse, the wrinkled skirt and my underwear, I rinsed every garment thoroughly in the sink. Sneaking back out into the bedroom butt naked, I retrieved some hangers from the Narnia wardrobe and hung my clothes to dry from the hooks in the bathroom. Then I slipped into the shower.

The water pressure wasn't all that impressive, but that shower might be one of the most wonderful experiences of my life.

Washing off all the grime with the complimentary shower gel, I remembered the car crash with a shudder. That could so easily have been the last mistake I had made. What a horrible way to go, swerving for a goat!

On a deep shelf across from the shower were folded up towels and two bathrobes arranged in an almost origami-like fold. I unshook one of them and slipped it on. The terrycloth was soft and luxurious, like something you would find in the best hotels in the world. And here I was, in a monastery in Italy. The idea made me laugh out loud. I was probably the last person who would ever consider joining a convent, and my friends would agree.

Rummaging through my tote, I found my phone and checked to see if Felicity or Laura had written anything in our Messenger group since this morning. But no. They were probably sleeping now, of course.

I put my bathing suit on and wrapped the sarong around my waist. With the cardigan on top, it almost looked like a proper outfit, but not quite. At least I wasn't naked. It would have to do until my clothes had dried.

I would have preferred to just stay here in my room and order room service, but there didn't seem to be a phone anywhere, and I didn't have the number for the reception. I couldn't even remember the name of the monastery. I would have to pick up a card from reception.

Walking back through the gardens, I stopped to admire the view once again. It looked completely different already, after less than an hour, and I imagined that it changed all the time, with the movement of the sun. I would have to work fast to capture it. And I intended to. But first, I needed to find something to eat. My stomach was growling.

The door to the kitchen was open and I peered inside. Marco was at the kitchen island, rinsing something under the tap. Something green. A vegetable of some sort, but I couldn't make out what kind from where I was standing. He placed the vegetables on a chopping board and grabbed a huge chef's knife. My eyes widened when I saw the large, sharp utensil move across the board at lightning speed.

A handyman? Oh, Heather, you shouldn't be so quick at jumping to conclusions.

I stared at his nimble fingers moving across the chopping board, handling that razor-sharp knife as if it was an extension of his hand. The green leaves were finely chopped and dropped into a pot over on the stove behind him. As he turned toward the stove, I climbed the stone steps and entered the kitchen. It was like watching an intricate choreography, the way he moved around his workspace, grabbing a bottle of olive oil and adding a dash to the pot, grabbing a spoon to stir the concoction, dipping a finger to taste and then adding salt and a variety of spices from the most elaborately stocked spice shelf I had ever seen.

I wasn't much of a cook, even though I certainly enjoyed good food, but the one thing I admired was skill. And Marco was truly skilled at what he was doing. I stared at his movements and wished I had something, a sketch pad and some charcoal ideally but a notepad and a biro, crayons and a flat wall, anything would do, just to capture the beautiful motions and lines that were happening right in front of me. It was unbelievable.

He was unbelievable.

I couldn't believe that I hadn't seen it from the start. That I had thought that he was just another man, a handyman that fixed things around the monastery.

No, he was *the chef.*

I couldn't reconcile that image with the one in my head, the one where he was out clearing weeds along the fence of the property, but that was just one of the ways in which he was contradictory. I had thought that he wasn't very strong, because there weren't any burly muscles in sight, but he had carried me from the car without batting an eyelid, and I was a big girl. I had thought that he wasn't very bright, but he spoke English with only the slightest of accents, and he was obviously trained in the culinary arts. I had seen master chefs at work in some of the world's finest restaurants, traveling with my grandfather, and I could tell that this man was not self-taught.

Moving closer to the kitchen island, I spotted the bucket he had brought with him for clearing the weeds. It was empty now. That was weird. Why had he brought that into the kitchen? Wasn't that terribly un-hygienic?

He suddenly noticed my presence and spun round.

"*Signorina* Heather. I didn't hear you come in," he said. Then he turned back to the stove and pulled the pot from the gas before facing me again. "Is the garden suite to your satisfaction."

I smiled. "It's perfect. Thank you." I glanced at the pot behind him before looking at his face again. "You didn't tell me that you were the chef."

He shrugged. "Are you hungry?"

I nodded eagerly. "Whatever that is, it smells divine."

He gestured at me to take a seat at the end of the kitchen island, where a couple of tall stools were pushed in underneath the table-top, and then busied himself with preparing a plate.

Just ladling up a portion of the soup into a large deep bowl wasn't enough. I watched with fascination as he garnished the soup with chunks of pork from a small frying pan on one of the back burners, croutons from another, and finally some herbs from a row of green plants in terracotta pots on the windowsill behind me.

When he presented me with the finished plate, I just stared at it in admiration. This wasn't a meal. It was a work of art. The pork cubes and the croutons weren't just dumped in the middle of the plate. Everything was arranged and thoughtfully stacked into the most aesthetically pleasing shapes possible.

He placed a large and heavy spoon next to my plate with a resonant clanging sound. It looked antique. I picked it up, but even though I was famished, I couldn't make myself destroy the beautiful arrangement.

"I had no idea," I said, forcing my eyes away from the bowl to look at him. He was standing right next to me, with an expectant look in his eyes. "Where did you learn to do this?"

"Try it," he said, instead of answering my question. "Eat, before it gets cold."

I reluctantly slipped the over-sized spoon into the edge of the soup and filled it without disturbing the intricate decorations in the middle of the bowl. I lifted the spoon to my lips and tasted it.

Heaven.

I didn't recognize the taste, something that surprised me, because I was no stranger to any of the world's cuisines, being well-traveled and well-fed since I was a little girl. But whatever it was, it was divine. The flavor was complex and layered and I let the soup roll back and forth over my tongue to get to all the nuances.

"Not just the soup," he said with a scolding voice. "Try it with everything."

I obediently but with regret tucked into his beautiful arrangement and filled the spoon with a little bit of everything, as instructed.

The soup had been an experience in and of itself but coupled with all these other flavors and textures, I was blown away. I had been hungry enough to just scarf down whatever had been put in front of me, especially since Marco had told me that they didn't serve lunch here, but this … This was an experience to be savored.

I took another spoonful, this time with my eyes closed, to really focus my attention. When I opened them again, he was staring at me, expectantly. This surprised me. If he was the chef, then he must cook for lots of people every day. Why did he care so much about what I thought about the food?

"Amazing," I said, almost breathlessly. "This is … otherworldly."

He shook his head. "No," he said, turning his back and busying himself with something on the stove. "No other world. Only *Toscana*."

I took another spoonful of the soup and thanked the goat for wandering out into the middle of the road.

4

MARCO

THE AMERICAN GIRL was sitting in my kitchen, eating my soup. This shouldn't mean a thing, but I still couldn't stop myself from staring at her when she took the first taste. The look on her face ...

There was something so attractive about a woman who enjoyed good food. Who enjoyed pleasurable experiences. Very appealing.

I forced my mind away from thoughts on what else a beautiful woman like that would like to experience on her visit to Italy and admonished her for only tasting the soup and not the garnishes. That was like looking at a beautiful painting with one eye closed.

She should know that. She was an artist. Or an art student, more likely. She was too young to be an accomplished artist.

Too young to be traveling alone through Italy.

Despite my best intentions, I kept an eye on her while she ate, noticing details that I did my very best not to memorize. The way she closed her eyes when she took another spoonful of soup, to focus her concentration on the flavor. The little moan of pleasure as she rolled the soup on her tongue. The way she tilted her head back, exposing her vulnerable neck and acres of soft, smooth skin all the way down into that exhilarating plunged neckline. For such a young girl, there was no doubt she was all woman, and I felt honored as a man to have stood above her while she ate, admiring those enticing orbs.

Admiration from afar was all right, I told myself. There was no harm in that. She was a sweet girl, and she couldn't possibly have any idea what went through a man's head when he saw someone like her up close. At least, I hoped not.

"Are you on holiday?" I asked her, as she finished the soup.

She put the spoon down and dabbed her lips with the cloth napkin I had laid out for her. "Sort of," she said. "I just graduated from college, a couple of weeks ago. My grandfather wanted me to come here and paint and study the masters. It's sort of a busman's holiday, I guess."

I leaned back against the work top and nodded. "Yes. People come to *Toscana* from all over the world to paint."

She glanced toward the door. "I can understand why. It's so beautiful here."

I cleared her plate. "Would you like anything else?"

She shook her head. "No, thank you. It was amazing, but I'm eager to get to work."

"Very well. Dinner is served at 8, in the formal dining room."

She glanced down. She had changed her clothes, and this new outfit was even less formal than the one she had been wearing before. Was that a bathing suit? The skirt was bright and colorful and way too sheer for comfort. *My* comfort, at least. Then she shrugged. "I'd better go and speak to the woman in reception about ordering some room service then."

I frowned. Of course. She hadn't brought any luggage and none of her outfits could be considered formal. "I'll take care of it," I said. "You get to work."

Her smile almost knocked me off my feet. Some of the staff here at the hotel used to complain about Americans and their fake smiles, but this was 100% genuine. It was obvious that she was passionate about her art.

"Thank you, again," she said, blasting me with the full wattage. "For saving me from those *dreadful* nettles, for sorting out the tow truck and the room. And for the unbelievable food." Her eyes widened. "I've never tasted anything like it. Might I ask what kind of soup that was?"

I gave her a crooked smile. "That was my renowned 'dreadful nettle soup'."

The look on her face was priceless, and I almost laughed out loud. But only almost. It had been a long time since I laughed out loud at anything at all.

She mumbled something that might have

been intended as an apology and left the kitchen.

THAT SAME EVENING, a couple of minutes past 8, I knocked on the door to her suite. In my other hand, I held a tray with *antipasto*. The guests in the dining room were being served nettle soup at this very moment, but since she had already had some, I had brought *signorina* Heather a platter of prosciutto, pecorino, some marinated mushrooms, and a small spring onion quiche, just large enough for two bites. Next to the plate was a small carafe of red wine and a glass of prosecco for the *Aperitivo*. Nothing much, just a little something to tide her over until the *primo piatto* was served in half an hour or so.

The door opened, and I could tell from the look on her face that she hadn't been expecting me. She was dressed in the hotel's bathrobe and had pinned her hair up in a messy bun that at least a third of the dark tresses had successfully escaped from. She had no makeup on and was probably not wearing anything underneath the terrycloth bathrobe. Still, she was the most beautiful woman I had ever seen. A sharp scent of paint thinner assaulted my nostrils. Underneath that, I could smell the complimentary bath soap that Elana bought in bulk for all the bathrooms here at the *monasterio*.

"M-m-marco?" she stuttered, and one hand flew up to make sure that the bathrobe stayed in place. "I … I wasn't expecting …"

She took a small step back and held up the door for me. I put the tray down on the small dining table and quickly set a place for her.

"You don't have to do that," she said, somewhere behind my right shoulder.

"*Nessum problema*," I said. "It is my pleasure."

She moved closer to the table. "It looks delicious," she said. "Is that honey, on the cheese?"

I nodded. "Yes. We keep some beehives here on the property."

Her eyebrows rose. "Did you sling it yourself? I'm impressed."

I wasn't sure what that meant. "*Il primo piatto* is served at 8.30. I'll bring it over."

She glanced down at the tray. "*Primo piatto?*"

"The first course," I explained. "Tonight, that is risotto."

She pursed her lips. "I'm looking forward to it." Glancing down at the tray, she continued. "Although, I could probably survive until breakfast on what you've already brought me." She picked up the wineglass and took a sip. "Yum," she said, putting the glass back down again. "Thank you."

I nodded. "I'll be back."

This provoked a chuckle from her.

"Okay, Arnold," she said, closing the door behind me.

"My name is Marco," I said, frowning.

I could hear her laughter through the closed door.

5

HEATHER

I COULDN'T BELIEVE my eyes when I opened the door and saw Marco standing there, looking all serious and gorgeous. The sky had gone pitch dark while I had showered and rested after a long and intense afternoon of painting, and a ridiculously large full moon hung just above his left shoulder. He was holding a tray filled with delicious little nibbles and treats and made a point of setting the table for me. He didn't say much while he was here, and he obviously didn't get my joke as he was leaving, but I was still surprised at my reaction to his short visit.

I don't know why my heart started racing

whenever he was around, and my skin went all tingly. Sure, I was naked underneath the bathrobe, after taking a second shower, but still.

It wasn't as if there was anything going on here. There was no flirting, no innuendos. He wasn't acting like a lot of other Italian men had done during my first weeks here, being very obvious in their appreciation. But on the other hand, I don't know why else he would take the time out of serving a four-course meal in the formal dining room to bring me food on a tray. Surely, he had staff who could do that for him. But then … as distant as he was, I had noticed him looking at me now and then, when he thought I wouldn't notice. Perhaps he was interested, after all?

Well, why the heck not? Sure, he was twice my age, at least, and I was only here for one night, but on the other hand, the girls would expect me to bring back tales of passionate Italians. A dreamy chef making passionate Italian love to me in a monastery would go over like a storm with Felicity and

Laura. Felicity would be scandalized and Laura jealous. Oh, I could hear them now. Grabbing my phone from the bedroom, I sat down to my elaborate starter plate and began to explore the different flavors while I checked our Messenger group. Still no new posts. None of the others were online. With a sigh I put the phone down and dug into the yummy food.

A couple of minutes past 8.30, there was another knock on the door. This time I was prepared. I opened the door with a welcoming smile (with perhaps a hint of seduction thrown in, just in case) and complimented him on the delicious honey.

"I'll tell the gardener," came his curt reply.

The risotto smelled divine, but I barely had time to tell Marco this before he was out the door. Well, that was disappointing! Perhaps I had misread the signs?

Alone again, I sat down and tried my best to enjoy the meal in solitude. The food was awesome, that wasn't the problem. The problem was that I missed my friends. I wasn't used to being alone and had never sought out my own company if I could avoid it. Coming to Italy was the first long trip I had ever taken on my own, and I wasn't planning on making a habit out of it. There was just something almost pathetic about not having anyone to share all these new experiences with.

I usually traveled with my grandfather, and occasionally with my parents. The next time I went anywhere, I might ask one of the girls to come with me, or both of them, for that matter.

This time, though, I'd had to go alone, and I knew that. Not just because I needed to focus on my art and spend so much time painting, but for my grandfather.

I sighed and put the fork down, staring at the darkness outside of the small window next to the door. He would have loved this place, but he had probably never known that something like this even existed. An old monastery wasn't at all his kind of hotel. He liked the Ritz or the Plaza, Raffles or Belmont. Elegant and classy establishments that all looked pretty much the same regardless of where in the world you happened to be. It was a great way to travel, but I somehow had a feeling that I had experienced more since I left Florence this morning than I had done traveling around the world with my grandfather a couple of times a year for more than ten years.

I would have loved to show him this place, though. Show him the view from the ornate garden, the peeling frescoes, this incredible risotto. I swallowed back the lump in my throat, lifting my face to the ceiling to stop the tears from welling up. It had been three months, but I still couldn't believe that he was gone. All my life, he had always been there. Loving, supporting, encouraging me in whatever I wanted to do.

Now, what was I supposed to do without him?

Keep going, I could hear him saying. Go out into the world and do great things. I know you can do it!

At graduation, I had kept looking out into the audience, searching for his face. It had felt so wrong that he hadn't been there. He had been there at every important event in my life, and always brought me a thoughtful gift. He had been widowed before I was born, and I was his only grandchild, so perhaps he had spoiled me a little, but that's what grandparents are for, right?

After the graduation ceremony, my mother had handed me an envelope with my name on it, in his handwriting. I had burst into tears, right then and there, surrounded by lots of people experiencing the happiest day of their life so far. It had been the strangest, most contradictory experience.

My darling Heather, he'd written. *Congratulations on your graduation. If you are reading this, I wasn't able to attend. But please don't be sad on this magnificent day. And whatever you do, don't spend your first summer as an adult grieving for an old man who lived a long and happy life. I want you to be happy and enjoy life, every precious day of it. And for you, this means painting. I always wanted you to study art where it all began, but you chose to stay at home and go to school in Seattle. Now, I'm asking you to please go to Florence and bring your paints. Stay there all summer! Study the masters and learn what you can from them. Then I want you to go out into the world and create beautiful art. Have the time of your life! Live and love, with no regrets!*

The letter was signed with his illegible scrawl of a signature. I had put it in my box of paints and carried it with me everywhere I went. I'm doing it, Papa, I thought. I'm here. I'm painting. I'm living. Or trying to. Loving, not so much.

The room suddenly felt cramped, and I got up and walked over to the window, flinging it open. There was a chill in the night air, and I just stood there for a while letting it cool my face. My eyes stung and the lump in my throat refused to budge. And on top of it all, the risotto was getting cold. Damn it, Heather!

I returned to the table and finished my meal. Even if it had gone cold, it was still the best risotto I had ever had. Marco had some serious kitchen skills.

In the corner of the room stood my easel with the painting I had been working on all afternoon. It was of the view from the garden, and I thought that I had done a pretty good job, but I was still eager for it to be morning so that I could go back outside and continue. If I got an early start, I might have time to make some sketches and snap some photos that I could use for more paintings. This place was certainly worth depicting. It had a timeless quality and a particular beauty to it.

By the time Marco knocked on the door again, I had calmed down, and he probably couldn't tell that I had been crying.

He had brought the *secondo piatto*, with turned out to be some kind of roast. On a separate plate was a variety of vegetables, and there was a small bowl with a sauce that smelled faintly of rosemary. He had also brought another carafe of that delicious red wine.

"Are you trying to get me drunk?" I joked to try and get him to reveal his intentions—or lack thereof. "There's really no need if you just want to take advantage. I'd rather be sober for that."

He glanced over at me where he stood by the table, shifting plates and bowls from the tray to the table, from the table to the tray, without even looking at what he was doing. "Excuse me?"

His lack of understanding was obvious. No intentions. It was disappointing, but at least now I knew. "Nothing," I said and walked over to him, looking down at the meal. "Thank you, again. It looks great."

He harrumphed a little. "Enjoy your meal," he said and walked toward the door.

"I'm sure I will," I said a little wistfully.

He stopped in the doorway, looking back at me. "I'll be back in half an hour or so with the *dolce*. Is there anything else you need?"

A hug, said the voice in the back of my head. *I need you to put your inconspicuously strong arms around me and comfort me all through the night in the way I'm sure that only a pure-blooded Italian male can do.*

I could feel the gravitational pull he exuded, apparently unintentionally, but held back. He wasn't interested in me. Hadn't shown any signs of attraction at all. And men were usually pretty obvious with girls like me. There was something about big breasts that made them forget their manners.

But not Marco. He had been the perfect gentleman since he rescued me from the car this morning, and here he was, alone in the dark with a young, practically naked woman, desperate for his attention, and he showed no signs of wanting to make a move.

I shook my head. "No, there's nothing."

And then he left.

MARCO

To keep going back out to the garden suite with every course was an excruciating form of torture, but I couldn't *not* go. I should have sent one of the servers, but Anna was out sick and there was no way I was going to let those slobbering mongrels Luca or Giuseppe anywhere near that enticing young woman.

Not that there wasn't a feral mongrel inside of me as well. But I kept it on a painfully short leash.

The painting that the signorina had been working on all afternoon stood in the corner of the room. It was an unsettling rendering of a view that I had known all my life. I had tried to pretend that I hadn't noticed it, but all I wanted to do was to just stare at it for hours. It was more or less the view from my own room on the third floor, but it was depicted in a way that I had never seen it, and the contrast between familiar and alien was disturbing. I quickly had to reevaluate the young woman's skills. This wasn't just some pretentious art student with delusions of grandeur. No. She was a true artist.

So young. So talented.

And so ... sad.

Yes, that was it. There had been an intense sadness in her eyes when I had returned with the *secondo piatto*. Perhaps she'd had some bad news from home? Her phone had been lying on the table, screen down thankfully. I hated the idea of her scrolling through social media while she ate. That was no way to enjoy a meal.

But then ... she was all alone. That was also no way to eat. Eating was a communal activity, and good food should be consumed with friends and family, so that you could share the experience. That was the whole point of food, of eating, as far as I was concerned. No one should ever have to eat alone, in solitude, far from your home and loved ones.

So, when I set the tray for *signorina* Heather's *dolce*, I told Giuseppe that he and Luca would have to manage the dining room on their own for the rest of the evening. Something had come up. His surprise was obvious, but he did his best to hide it. I never left them in charge, especially not when Anna wasn't around to keep an eye on them. I was always here, always watching, always the one in control. Delegation was not something that I was particularly good at. But it was just for one night, I kept telling myself. I had already saved the beautiful *signorina* once today. Now I needed to save her again, from an evening of sadness and solitude.

Balancing the tray on my fingertips, I made my way back through the garden for the fourth time this evening. The night was anything but silent, even though the dining room was on the other side of the massive stone building. The cicadas kept going long into the night, and there were rustling and scrabbling noises coming from the bushes. I glanced over into the darkness on the other side of the garden wall, but there was barely anything to be seen of the view this late. Some lights from the village across the valley, and in the distance a car's headlights moved slowly along a winding road. Giacomo would come tomorrow and sort out the young *signorina's* car, and then I would never see her again.

It shouldn't bother me. But it did.

What was it about this young woman?

I barely had time to knock on the door before it opened. She had been expecting me.

She had finished all the food and most of the wine. Perhaps that was why she seemed more relaxed this time around. The phone was still lying in exactly the same place on the table as before. Perhaps she hadn't even touched it? The thought pleased me more than it should.

She followed me over to the table and leaned forward to study the contents of the tray I had brought her. This evening's *dolce* consisted of a chocolate panna cotta and an assortment of exotic fruits cut into decorative shapes. Luca's work. The youngster was quite skilled with a paring knife. But the panna cotta was my own recipe, and I had made it myself. I had brought enough for both of us but seeing the way her bathrobe opened when she leaned forward over the table, I instantly regretted that decision.

Too late. She looked up at me with eyes that glowed with something that was both stimulating and frightening all at once.

"Are you joining me for dessert, Marco?"

I nodded. As soon as I had cleared away the plates from the previous course, I pulled out her chair. Her smile as she sat down lit up the room. The view I got from standing over her chair made me dizzy. This had been a bad idea, but there was no turning back now. I could do this, I kept telling myself. I would have some panna cotta with the American *signorina*. Make some polite conversation. Tell her about the *monasterio* and its history. That was not a problem. I had told the story enough times to tourists from all around the world.

I poured her the *digestivo* and she sipped it carefully. There was a slight grimace as she noticed how strong it was, but then an appreciative smile spread on her naturally red lips.

"Wonderful," she proclaimed and put her glass back down. Then she waited for me to take a seat before picking up the spoon and sampling the panna cotta. I watched her face as she explored the texture and all the flavors. It was an intense experience; I knew that. People had told me, often, that I made the best panna cotta in all of Italy. That probably wasn't true. But it was up there, among the best. I picked up my own spoon and tasted it.

It didn't matter that I had made it myself and that I had tasted it while I made it to make sure that I got the flavors just right. It didn't matter that I had made this dish thousands of times over the years. I never got tired of food. Every time you prepared a dish was like the first time. There was always something different, some new discovery. Like making love to a beautiful woman was never the same from time to time. If you loved her, you never became bored with her body, her voice, her caresses. Food was also like that. There was always satisfaction to be had if you put the effort in during the preparations.

And the best part of eating good food was seeing the people around you share your experience. Seeing the pleasure that the young *signorina* got from the panna cotta was almost better than tasting the smooth chocolate dessert myself. It was obvious that she liked it, and I couldn't stop looking at her face. Her beauty wasn't perhaps of the classical variety, but there was no man on earth who wouldn't consider her a masterpiece. That face, that body, the way her lips closed on the dessert spoon … Oh, she would make some man very happy one day.

She looked up and our eyes met over the table.

"Thank you," she said, her voice a little hoarse. "I really needed some company tonight."

I nodded. "My pleasure."

She shook her head slowly. "No, decidedly not."

The way she was looking at me was disconcerting. I couldn't stand what was happening in my body when we stared into each other's eyes, so I forced myself to look away. The painting was standing at the perfect angle from where I was sitting.

"Your painting, it is amazing," I said. "You are very talented for someone so young."

She barely glanced at the painting. "Thanks," she said, as if it was nothing. "It needs a lot more work."

I leaned forward. "Don't disrespect your gift."

She looked surprised. "I … don't think that's what I did." She looked over at the painting again, properly this time. "It's just that I don't think of my painting as a talent or a gift. All I see whenever I look at something I drew or painted is all the hard work I put into it."

I studied her. "Has anyone ever told you that you are a very impressive young woman?"

Instead of thanking me for the subtle compliment, she burst into tears. I don't know what I had expected, but certainly not this. And it wasn't just a tiny teardrop down her smooth cheek. No. Her whole body suddenly shook with violent sobs and her large eyes flooded with tears that streamed down her naked face.

"W-was it something I said?" I asked. "If so, I am so terribly sorry. I didn't mean to …"

She used her cloth napkin to mop up some of the tears, and I could see her struggle to get the sobs under control. "It's just …" she sobbed. "I'm …" She buried her face in the crook of her arm for a moment. Then she pulled herself tall and blinked rapidly with her face turned toward the ceiling.

I felt like an idiot, just sitting there, watching her fall apart, but I knew that I couldn't go to her. There was nothing I could say or do what would offer her any consolation, and if I came too close, there was no telling what my inner mongrel would do.

I stood up, abruptly, and started to clear the table. "I should go," I muttered. "It is clear that I have upset you. Please forgive me. That was never my intention." I reached for her empty wine glass, and she grabbed my hand.

"It's not your fault," she said, smiling bravely but still with large round tears glistening in her thick lashes. "Please don't go." She stood up, without releasing my hand.

"I must," I said brusquely. Oh, I absolutely had to get out of there. Every part of my body was aching to wrap my arms around her and comfort her, even though I had no idea what had made her so upset. A violently protective instinct that I hadn't known that I possessed flared up inside of me, and I wanted to kill the man who had broken her heart. Because that had to be the reason for her sadness, surely? Why else would she be all alone here in Italy?

"Please don't," she said again, her voice no more than a whisper. She pulled my hand towards her, clutching it to her chest. The edge of my little finger touched the naked skin above her plunging cleavage, and it seared my hand as if I had pressed it against a grill. As with all chefs, the skin on my hands was like asbestos and I could easily handle things that I had just pulled from the oven, but her bare chest made my skin sizzle in a way I had never experienced before. Oh, lord, please help me. I can't. I mustn't. I absolutely have to leave here. Now.

She took a step closer, turning my hand and pressing it flat against her chest. I could feel her heart thudding against my palm. It was fast, but not anywhere near the frantic pace of my own. If there was a pressure gauge somewhere in my brain, it would be showing red now. I was overheating. On the verge of exploding.

I had to get out of here before someone got hurt.

"Please don't leave," she whispered, turning her face up toward me, inviting a kiss, inviting me to … I couldn't even imagine what she might be offering. It was all so surreal. She was so young. So beautiful. So talented.

She had no business offering up her incredible body to an old pathetic creature like me. It would be a crime. Perhaps not illegal, but still … a crime.

Images of all the things I wanted to do to her flashed before my mind's eye, and I pulled away from her with a violent tug, staggering backward toward the door. The temptation was too great.

I had to get out of here before I did something that *signorina* Heather was going to regret.

HEATHER

THE DOOR SLAMMED SHUT behind Marco and I just stood there, staring at it, listening to his footsteps moving away across the gravel outside. My chest was heaving, my eyes burning and my whole body was in uproar. There were too many emotions going on for one little heart to cope with and my chest felt as if it would burst open, letting it all out. I was devastated. Crushed. Humiliated.

Turning around, I regarded the small dining table, wondering what had happened here. Just a moment ago, we had been sitting there, together, enjoying the most amazing panna cotta I'd ever had. It had been so kind of Marco to join me for dessert, and I had assumed that …

Yes, what had I assumed?

That he would want to take me to bed?

God, Heather, how stupid are you? Just because a man is nice to you doesn't mean that he wants to have sex.

Well … Most of the time, that's exactly what it means.

I walked over to the table. We had finished all the food and all the wine. There was some of that booze left in the smaller carafe, though. I ignored the small glass he had served it in and poured all of it into my wine glass. It was rocket-fuel strong, but that would be exactly what I needed to get to sleep after the day I'd had. Not that I wasn't tired. Not at all. I was exhausted. But my mind and my body were in turmoil, and I didn't know how to unwind from it all.

I took a big sip of the strong liqueur and grimaced. Grabbing my phone, I took one last glance at my painting and then staggered into the bedroom. The girls were still not online, and I didn't bother with any other social media. This was not a moment to post about! Another big gulp and then I crawled under the covers. The sheets were cold against my bare skin, so I kept the bathrobe on. I curled up into a ball, turned out the lights and lay there, staring at the starry sky outside of the window. Perhaps I should have pulled the curtains, but I couldn't be bothered to get out of bed. I grabbed my glass from the bedside table and drained its contents. The warmth from the alcohol spread throughout my body. A last sob escaped me, and I rolled over, facing the wall. How could I have been so stupid? Thrown myself at a complete stranger like that? It was humiliating. Utterly, unreservedly humiliating. I would never be able to look Marco in the eye again.

But I probably wouldn't ever have to see him again. The chef didn't serve breakfast, surely. And before tomorrow night, the tow truck would have pulled my car out of the ditch and I would be back in Florence. I still had a whole summer of Italian adventures planned, and hopefully these adventures would involve at least one nice young man who would do his best to wipe this unfortunate and embarrassing experience from my mind.

I tried to picture this hypothetical Italian stallion, but memories of Marco kept crowding into my fantasies. His strong arms carrying me as if I were weightless. His dark eyes locking onto mine and creating a connection … a connection that had felt so real, it had fooled me into believing that he might feel it too. Stupid of me. He probably only saw me as a little girl. A helpless kid lost in the world. That was all it was. He had tried to be nice, and I had misunderstood his concern.

What would a man like that see in a girl like me?

His black eyes haunted me all the way into my dreams.

<hr>

THE SUN WOKE ME EARLY, thanks to the undrawn curtains. Despite my heavy head, I dragged myself out of bed and got ready. I only had a few precious hours to paint, and I had to make the most of it. I would never return to this place, unfortunately. This would be my only chance to capture the scenery around here.

I set up my easel in the garden, in approximately the same spot as yesterday, but the light was completely different at this time of day, and I didn't want to ruin my painting by messing up the colors. Instead, I snapped some photos and pulled out my large sketch pad. Moving around the garden, I made a number of sketches capturing details of the building and some of the garden features. By the time I had filled all the remaining pages, my stomach was growling. Unbelievable! After the substantial four-course dinner I'd had last night, I had planned on skipping breakfast, but the growls were distracting, and I had trouble focusing on the task at hand when all I could think about was food. And coffee! I desperately needed something to give me a little boost today.

Marco had worked late, so he was probably at home asleep. I could sneak into the breakfast room and grab some breakfast, and still have time to work on my second canvas before I had to leave.

The long corridor was silent and empty, but I could hear the distinctive sounds of people having breakfast coming from a room up ahead. I forced myself to remain calm and walked up to the door. It was a large room, facing east so that the sun poured in through the tall, narrow windows. Two long tables took up a large part of the floor space, with chairs down both sides. Only about half a dozen or so of the chairs were taken. It was still early. A young man in a dashing white chef's jacket was refilling a large covered serving dish, and a middle-aged woman in an apron was pouring coffee for some of the guests at the table to my right. Marco wasn't anywhere to be seen. I could feel some of the tensions from last night draining from my body. It was fine. He wasn't here. I would not have to face him.

I made my way over to the buffet table at the far end of the room. It was piled high with all kinds of breakfast things. Everything from rustic sourdough bread to airy crois-sants. Fruits and jams, cheeses and hams, ce-real and yogurts, bacon and eggs, and sausages. I took a plate and filled it with my favorites and some of the things that I didn't recognize. At the end of the table was a hot-plate with coffee and I filled a tall mug.

All the other guests were seated in small groups, clearly couples or families or friends, and I felt a little stupid sitting down all alone at one end of the table. I smiled at the nearest guests and then focused on the food. It was delicious, but after the first few bites, I found it difficult to focus on the flavors. Biting into the sandwich, I couldn't help but wonder if Marco had baked the bread. If he had sliced this ham. Was he around, after all? Back there in the kitchen?

I could feel my cheeks flushing at the idea of meeting him, trying to explain, having to apologize for ruining the evening. After the night I'd had, I just wasn't up to it.

Leaving food on the plate was not some-thing I was known for, but this was no normal day. I stood up abruptly, my chair scraping against the flagstone floor, grabbed the coffee mug and more or less bolted from the room.

I made it back out into the garden without running into any tall, handsome

Italian men and returned to my easel. Taking out the second canvas I had brought from the holder in the lid of my painter's box, I attached it to the easel. After all my sketching I knew exactly what I wanted to paint this time. I turned the easel around, so that I stood facing the monastery. The sun had just come round the corner of the garden annex and created slanting shadows across the ancient facade, all the way from the garden greenery up to the campanile. I made a quick composition sketch with light pencil marks, just to make sure that I had room for everything I wanted to capture, but then I got started on mixing colors. I wouldn't have time to finish this painting, but I wanted to make sure that I found the right colors and angles while I was here. Then, I could work from photos later.

The brown of the brick facade was pretty easy to figure out, but the shadows and the ivy in the corner kept coming out too dark. When I added more white, the colors became washed out. By the time I had finally figured it out, the sun was high in the sky, and I was beginning to feel stressed. I wasn't sure what bothered me the most, the fact that Marco would come to work any minute and might open that door to the kitchen over there, or that the guy with the tow truck might show up with my car before I had figured out the right shade of pink for the flowers along the garden path. But I was tense, that was obvious, and when someone appeared in a doorway over to one side and called out to me, I almost jumped out of my skin.

It was the receptionist from yesterday.

"*Signorina?*" she said, stepping down the two stone steps onto the garden path. "Giacomo is here. From the garage."

I put my brush down. "Has he managed to retrieve my car?"

She shook her head. "Not yet. He asks, please can he have the car key?"

Of course. I rummaged through my tote bag and found it, handing it over to her. "Does he think it will take long; do you know?"

She smiled at me. "He say, probably half an hour."

I glanced at my painting and then smiled back at her. "Great. Half an hour. I'll be here."

She nodded and disappeared back inside the building.

I looked around the garden. This was it. Another thirty minutes. If there was anything here that I wanted to paint, I needed to capture it now, with my camera or with a sketch. Preferably both. Looking over toward the garden wall, I could see that the light over the valley was once again completely different from all the other times I had seen it. I pulled out my phone and snapped some more photos, well aware of the fact that not even my iPhone would be able to capture those exact nuances. I would have to rely on my memory for those. If I ever managed to replicate them, that is. It wouldn't be easy.

Returning to my easel, I picked up my brush and added some strokes to the edge of the roof. There was something about the angle of it that wasn't quite right, but it was too late to do anything about it now. With a sigh, I grabbed a rag and started to wipe the paint off my brushes. I might as well pack up. My time at *Monasterio de Camillo* was up.

The door to the corridor opened again,

but this time it wasn't the receptionist. A tiny woman in a stern moss-green dress and a severe frown stepped gingerly down onto the path and came toward me with determined steps. I put away my brushes and was just about to loosen the screws that held my canvas in place when she came up to me, saying something in Italian.

"I'm sorry," I said. "I don't speak Italian."

The woman didn't seem to understand or care, because she kept talking, more and more and seemingly faster and faster. I only knew a few words of Italian and couldn't pick out any one of them from the flood of words that poured from the old woman's wrinkled old lips. She was gesticulating aggressively, and even though I couldn't understand a word she was saying, I got the message. She was *not* happy with me being here, with my paintings, or with anything to do with me.

"I'm sorry," I repeated, removing my canvas from the easel and stooping to put it in my painter's box. "But I'm leaving now. I'm going, I'm going." The woman bent down next to me and yanked the canvas from my hand, staring at it, and then gesticulating some more.

"Hey," I said. "Give me that."

The woman's gestures became even more animated. She bent down and turned my painter's box toward her.

"No," I said, "Leave that alone. Those are my—"

The woman found my other canvas, the painting from yesterday, and pulled it out of its slot in the lid of the box. I tried to take it back, but she was surprisingly strong for someone so tiny. Her head didn't even reach my shoulder, but she was fierce and very intimidating.

"Give me back my paintings!" I exclaimed, but the woman didn't listen. Instead, she turned and hurried back inside on her short legs. I ran after her.

A couple of guests were in the corridor and they stared at us as we careened past them, all the way to the reception area on the other side of the building. Thankfully, the English-speaking receptionist was there, behind the counter. She smiled at me as I stormed in through the doorway and held out my car key toward me.

"Good news, *signorina*. Giacomo has retrieved your car, and he says that there is no damage. He did not have to take it to the garage. It is in the parking lot out front. Here is your key."

The old woman had stopped in front of the counter and launched into another tirade, this time not directed at me, thankfully. I tried to get my paintings back, but she refused to let go of them.

"Can you please talk to her?" I said between gritted teeth, tugging at the edge of the larger canvas. "Tell her to give me back my paintings."

The receptionist looked surprised. Her eyes darted back and forth between the little old woman and me. When there was a slight pause in the elderly art thief's tirade, she replied in some rapid-fire Italian of her own. The old woman responded, and the receptionist smiled.

"She say, she wants to buy your paintings," she said to me. "She say, they are very good."

I stared at the little old woman. "They're not for sale," I said emphatically. "They're not even finished. Heck, I barely even started that second one."

The old woman burst into talking again, holding up my paintings against the wall opposite the reception desk.

"She say, you will make more painting. Make five painting, and we will have postcards made and sell here in reception."

"Postcards?" I frowned. What was she on about? I turned toward the receptionist. "Who *is* this woman?"

The receptionist smiled. "This is *signora* Balducci," she said, as if that explained anything. When I shrugged, she continued. "She own *Monasterio de* —"

I glanced at the old woman. "She is the owner? But ..." I shook my head. "It doesn't matter. My paintings are not for sale. And I certainly don't want them made into postcards." So tacky. I was not that kind of artist!

"That is too bad," the receptionist replied with a sad face. "*Signora* Balducci say, all our guests will want to buy prints of these paintings and send postcards to all their friends."

I snorted. "I don't care. My paintings are not for sale."

The *signora* came up to me, a little bit too close for comfort, and continued her ceaseless tirade. The receptionist translated. "She ask, how much for five paintings like these?"

"It's not about the money," I protested.

The receptionist translated my reply. The old woman cackled and said something back that sounded as if she didn't believe me. The receptionist smiled apologetically as she translated her reply, "She say, you are young art student. Need money. All student need money."

I tried to protest, but the woman continued. This time with one index finger stabbing at my nose.

"She say," the receptionist said, "how long to paint five paintings like these?"

I shook my head in bewilderment. "I … I don't know. At least a week." I turned toward the receptionist. "But I can't stay. I have to get back to Florence. I need to return my rental car today. I only hired it for two days."

After a quick translation back and forth, the receptionist turned toward me again.

"She say, fine. Go to Firenze. Return car. But then you come back here. Stay a week. She will pay, and you will paint the *Monasterio,* five paintings as beautiful as these. She will have prints made and postcards and perhaps even pillows. Our guests will want to buy these and bring them home. Your art will be in homes all around the world."

Part of me wanted to just tear my paintings from the old woman's grip and flee to my car outside. This was insanity, and my head was splitting from all the angry Italian that had been directed toward me during the past ten minutes. If the woman loved my paintings so much, why did she seem so angry?

And then there was … Marco. Even if the idea of my art in homes around the world and on postcards had appealed to me, a week here at the monastery would surely mean that I would run into him again. And that meant humiliation with a capital H.

With a final, determined tug, I wrenched my unfinished canvases from the old woman's hands. "Once I've returned the car,

I won't be able to come back here," I said. "Now, if you'll excuse me, I'm leaving."

I was almost out the door when another smattering of angry Italian assaulted me from behind. "The *signora* say, you will never be able to finish your painting if you leave. The view of the valley, is tricky. Because of light. Very special light."

I stopped in the doorway, refusing to turn around. Glancing down at the painting from yesterday, I felt a pang as I realized that she was right. Not even with the help of all the photos I had taken, all the sketches I had made, would I ever be able to make that marvelous view justice.

As soon as I left here, my memories would begin to fade. And in some parts, that would be an immense relief. But in others …

It would haunt me for the rest of my life, that unfinished painting, I knew that.

Slowly, I turned around. The little old lady looked satisfied. When she spoke again, it was a little more calmly, but still with the same determination.

"She say," the receptionist translated automatically, "you go to Firenze, return car, pack a bag. Then, her son will collect you this evening and bring you back. You will stay here one week, and paint five paintings. She will pay you."

If it hadn't been for Marco, I would have jumped at the opportunity to stay here and paint for a whole week. And in the end, that was what made me decide. I did not want to be the kind of woman who missed out on something like this, an opportunity of a lifetime, because of some guy. I would stay in the garden flat. He would avoid me like the plague, once he heard that I was back, of that I was sure. If I ordered room service, he would surely send someone else with the tray.

"All right," I said, with a heavy sigh. "I will come back here."

8

MARCO

I HAD SLEPT POORLY and awoke at the crack of dawn, feeling just as tired as I had been when I went to bed. Perhaps even more. What a dreadful, dreadful evening that had been.

It was my own fault for going out there like that. For getting too close.

I should have known better.

I *had* known better. But I hadn't listened to reason, hadn't cared about what might happen.

And that had almost been my downfall.

My living room on the third floor was flooded by the early morning sun when I came out of my bedroom. I walked over to the small kitchenette I had installed when I moved back and made myself an espresso. My usual morning routine consisted of going for a walk down the valley, but this morning I didn't feel like going outside, for some reason. I wouldn't start work for several hours and was feeling weirdly restless. Walking over to the window, I looked down into the garden.

And there she was.

Unbelievable. It was barely past 7 in the morning, but it looked as if she had been out there for hours. She was completely absorbed by her sketch pad and her hand made determined strokes across the large sheath of paper. She worked with an intense energy and determination, and it was mesmerizing to watch. The way she moved around the garden, crossing the lawn at an angle, strolling along the path, it was like a beautifully choreographed dance performance. I could watch her for hours.

Suddenly, she turned and stared up at the facade. It was as if she looked straight at me, and I instinctively took a couple of steps back. Had she seen me? She couldn't have.

Slowly, I approached the window again, from an angle, so that I could peer down at her without being seen. She was completely absorbed by her sketch. It didn't seem that she had noticed me up here.

When she returned to her easel, turning it to face the building, I knew that I had to get out of here. If I didn't leave, I would spend all morning lurking behind the curtains, staring at her, and that would quickly drive a man insane. I found my car keys and made my way down the stairs, hurrying out to the parking lot. There was a fish market a couple of towns over where I didn't usually go, because it was too far and it took all morning, but today, that was exactly what I needed.

By the time I got back, *la bella signorina Americana* would have left, and my life could get back to normal again.

THE FISH MARKET had been a tumultuous affair, and I had spent way too much money on some crayfish that I didn't know what I wanted to do with, but by the time I got back, it was early afternoon and I felt confident that she'd be gone.

And she was. The receptionist told me that Giacomo had been able to get the car back up on the road without any trouble and *la signorina Americana* had gone back to Firenze.

I didn't like the feeling in my chest when she delivered that last piece of information. Not one bit. Surely, I was relieved that *signorina* Heather was gone, and that there would be no more distractions. Women. There was no room for them in my life. It was better this way.

But when I walked into the kitchen, another woman was standing right there, by my stove. She was stirring something that smelled appalling. My heart sank.

"*Buon giorno, Mama*," I said, handing the boxes of seafood to Luka, who took them into the walk-in fridge.

"Marco," my mother said, without looking up from whatever she was making. "I need you to do something for me."

I felt the weight of her expectations and disappointments pressing down on my shoulders, as always when my mother came by. "Certainly, *Mama*."

"You will go to Firenze this evening," she continued, grabbing some herbs from my flowerpots and dropping them in her concoction. "I've commissioned a young artist to make some paintings of the *monasterio*. It is Sergio's night off, so you will have to drive."

I stared at her. Surely not. It couldn't be. "A young artist?" I croaked. It had to be a coincidence. Someone she had met at a party or something. A handsome young man. My mother loved going to parties and flirting with handsome young men. It was disgusting. "What young artist? What are you talking about?"

"Oh, the most marvelous young woman." My heart sank so fast it hit the flagstone floor with a splat. "She was staying here in the garden suite; can you believe it. She was outside in the garden this morning, painting. A most amazingly talented girl. I hired her on the spot." She launched into one of her tirades about what a great opportunity this was, but I didn't hear a word of it. The realization of what her words meant hit me like an anvil, dropped from a substantial height.

"No, *Mama*," I protested. There were so many reasons why this wasn't going to work. "You can't hire an artist. We can't afford something frivolous like that. We've got actual bills to pay. The roof needs to be—"

She interrupted me. "This girl is very talented. Her paintings will *make* us money, not cost us money."

Getting my mother to listen to reason was like … I don't know. Getting *signor* Vitello's cows to wash the dishes for me. No matter how hard I tried, it could only end badly. "No, *Mama*," I said with a heavy sigh. "Maybe they will, someday, but for now, they will be an expense. And it's an expense that we don't need and can't afford."

She waved my objections away with a dismissive gesture. "You have to think of the future, Marco *mio*," she said. "Make plans. Try new things."

I didn't reply. This was the same argument we'd had for ten years, and I did not want to get into it again. I didn't want to make any plans. I didn't want to try new things. I had plenty of old things that I still needed to deal with and process. Maybe someday, I would be done with the past and able to move on.

But not today.

And the idea of *signorina* Heather returning to the *monasterio* for a whole week … No, no, no. Absolutely not. Under no circumstances. This could only end badly.

I walked toward the door with determined steps. "Well, I'm not going to Firenze," I said. "You'll have to get someone else to do it. I won't go. *Basta!*"

AT 8 PM, sharp, I rang the doorbell of the AirBnb where *signorina* Heather was staying. Mothers. There was no arguing with them. And here I was.

The door opened, and there *she* was. The shock on her face when she saw me standing there was obvious, and so was the discomfort that replaced it just a split second later.

"Marco," she exclaimed, and her voice sounded faint.

"*Signorina* Heather," I said, doing my best to sound formal and courteous. It wasn't easy. My body was reacting violently to being this close to her again, and I had to use all my self-control to keep from sweeping her into my arms and take some of what she may or may not have offered me last night.

This evening, she was nothing like last night, though. She was properly dressed, for one, in a lovely dress that made the absolute most out of her magnificent body. It was a pale shade of purple and had lots of layers and beads and embroideries. It should have looked hippie-ish and ridiculous, but instead, it made her look intensely feminine and exotic. Her face was made up, and her thick dark hair was pinned up in a messy bun, leaving her long, slender neck bare. I suddenly understood where that whole thing about vampires had come from, because the urge to bury my teeth in that soft, vulnerable skin was animalistic and aggressive.

"W-what are you doing here?" she asked, and I could see that she was struggling to compose herself. Her fingers fidgeted with the buttons at the end of her sleeve. "*Signora*

Balducci said that she would send her s—"
Her eyes widened when she put two and two
together. "*You* are her son," she said, her
voice barely more than a whisper.

I nodded sternly. "For my sins," I said and
regretted it instantly. I did not want to talk
about sins, not even think about sins, anywhere near this beautiful and innocent creature. That way madness lay. "Are you ready
to go?"

She glanced at a small suitcase standing
right by the door, next to her large painter's
box and a sizeable shopping bag from an art
supply store containing a number of blank
canvases. I leaned forward and picked up the
painter's box and the suitcase, gesturing toward the stairs.

"My car is right outside," I said when she
still didn't move.

She hesitated a while longer, too long for
me to be able to pretend that I didn't notice. I
forced myself to look indifferent but didn't
know what I'd do if she refused to go. It
would be a relief, but at the same time …

In the end, she grabbed the bag of blank
canvases and closed the door behind her,

tugging the handle to make sure that it had locked properly. She walked ahead of me down the stairs and out into the street.

It was a nice enough neighborhood if you wanted to be in the middle of it all. The constant noise of people, cars, and just life, in general, would have driven me mad if I'd had to stay here any length of time, though. I had been right to return to the *monasterio*, after …

No. Not going to think about that now. This was difficult enough, without me opening the closet and letting all my skeletons out to play. The *signorina's* curvy hips swayed from side to side as we walked over to where I had parked the car, and even though I did my very best to look away, my eyes were constantly drawn to her hypnotizing movements. Her beauty was of a magnificently opulent kind that whetted my appetites in a way that I hadn't experienced for so long. I had thought that I would never feel this way ever again. I had been convinced that this part of my life was over. That I would never find another woman who would make me feel anything like this.

There could never be another woman like Giulietta.

I stopped in the middle of the street, putting the suitcase down and fumbling for the car fob. I hadn't spoken Giulietta's name since it happened, hadn't even thought it to myself. Doing it now, here in the street with *signorina* Heather, felt wrong on so many levels. I had felt like a mongrel for lusting after *la bella signorina Americana*, but this was worse. I was actually comparing this young woman to Giulietta. And that was just … not okay.

I walked over to the car and placed her luggage in the trunk, resting for a moment with my hand on the warm metal to gather my wits, what little there was left of them. What was it about this frighteningly young foreigner that made me react so violently? She was just a girl, probably not even half my age.

Giulietta would have laughed at me, calling me a dirty old man. I closed my hand around the car key and pressed the jagged edge into my flesh to try and distract myself from the even worse pain that clawed at my chest. Fight fire with fire, wasn't that what they said, *gli Americani?* Dull emotional pain with a purely physical one. Physical pain I could handle. The emotional suffering, that's where I was brought to my knees, over and over.

A part of my ridiculous brain wondered if *la bella signorina* might be able to provide some relief from that suffering, but I refused to even consider it. That would be the ultimate betrayal of Giulietta, to soothe my grief for her with another woman. With some random stranger that didn't mean anything.

And no other woman could ever mean anything to me.

I wasn't going to let anyone close enough for that kind of connection. Never again.

I had to force myself to move over to the driver's side, and sliding in behind the steering wheel, I held my breath for as long as I could, to avoid being overwhelmed by *signorina* Heather's presence, her scent, her … being there. The car was big but nowhere near big enough, and not even the lingering stench of fish from this morning seemed to dull my reaction to being near her.

9

HEATHER

I COULDN'T BELIEVE my eyes when I opened the door and saw him standing there. I had known all along that it had been a mistake to accept *signora* Balducci's offer, and here was the confirmation. There was no way I was going to be able to avoid Marco this week. I hadn't even made it back to the monastery yet, and here we were. Sitting close together in his car, speeding through the darkness.

Despite the madness on the Autostrada, I felt completely safe sitting next to him. He operated the car like he did his pots and pans and kitchen utensils, with a smooth and professional touch that made it seem perfectly effortless. It was a thing of beauty and utterly stimulating to watch.

No matter how hard I tried, I couldn't keep my eyes off him. At least it was dark inside the car, so he probably didn't notice me looking. He would be embarrassed if he did, I'm sure. It was obvious that he didn't want to be here, but he must have found *signora* Balducci as impossible to reason with as I had. That poor man. I couldn't imagine what it was like to have a mother like that.

Not that an absent mother like mine was any great trophy.

I forced my hungry eyes away from Marco and stared out into the darkness.

Perhaps that had something to do with it. I had always suspected that my lack of close relationships with my parental units was the reason for my many romantic entanglements, but none of the boys that I had used to try and fill the void inside my heart had been anything like Marco. They had all been just that, boys.

Marco was very much a man, and I finally understood the difference.

Too bad that he saw me as a girl, someone that he could never be attracted to.

I just had to be professional. Do the job that his mother had hired me to do, keep out of his way, and then get on with my life.

One week.

That time would just fly by once I got started on my paintings; I was sure of that. It always did when I was working.

It had been dark when we left Florence, but with all the lights in the city, I hadn't really noticed it. When Marco pulled into the parking lot in front of the monastery, the sky was pitch black and sprinkled with stars. An almost full moon hung over the valley. It looked closer than I had ever seen it before, and I could make out shadows and details on the surface. I stepped out of the car and just stood there, listening to the engine ticking as it cooled down, staring at the night sky. Compared to the commotion in the city, this was heaven. So quiet. So tranquil. The chilly night air was perfumed by a million unfamiliar scents, all of them pleasant.

Steps across the gravel told me that Marco had walked around to get my luggage out of the trunk. I swiveled and hurried up to him.

"I'll get it," I said, reaching for the handle of the suitcase at the same time as he leaned forward to grab it. I walked straight into his shoulder and he reacted as if I had pressed a branding iron against his flesh, jerking back.

The embarrassment from when I had humiliated myself last night flared up again, with an additional burning shame that he would be so repulsed by my body that he couldn't stand even an accidental touch. My cheeks burned and I turned my head away from the small light inside of the trunk so that he wouldn't see how much he had hurt my feelings.

"I will carry your luggage for you," he said curtly and picked it up as if it weighed nothing at all. I knew for a fact that it weighed quite a lot, but you couldn't tell by looking at him.

"There's no need," I said. "I know the way.

Signora Balducci said that I was to stay in the garden suite."

"But you don't have the key," he said.

I looked down at my shoes. That was true.

He slammed the trunk shut and walked ahead of me toward the door to the reception.

There was no one there, but he walked behind the counter and fetched the key with the large marker, handing it to me.

"Thank you," I said, reaching for my bags, but he wouldn't hand them over. He just nodded in the direction of the corridor toward the garden. With a sigh, I walked ahead of him.

The whole place seemed deserted. That was strange. It wasn't that late and there were plenty of guests staying here. But I was glad that no one saw my humiliating return. And since one of the reasons that my suitcase was so heavy was because it contained enough snacks, beverages and treats for me to not have to leave the garden suite all week, I figured the worst was behind me.

Walking past the rosemary bush, I tried

to push all the unpleasant emotions to the side and just revel in the fact that I was back. I was here and I had an entire week to paint. Commissioned paintings that might end up in Japan or South Africa or … Seattle, for that matter. That was so cool, and if I could just get over this silly crush on Marco, this could turn out to be the most awesome adventure ever. I just graduated two weeks ago, and here I was, working on my first commission as a professional artist, in Italy!

You rock, Heather! I told myself, as I walked through the archway and found the door to the garden suite. The key slipped effortlessly into the lock and I let myself in, leaving the door open for Marco. On the table was a fruit basket and a bottle of wine. I walked over and pulled the card out of the basket. The writing was in Italian and the signature may or may not have said *signora* Balducci.

Marco came in through the door and put my luggage down. I held out the card toward him. "I think it's from your mother. What does it say?"

He glanced at it. "It says that you are welcome and that she hopes you will have a nice time."

I smiled. "Thank her for me, if you see her."

He frowned. "She's gone to *Roma* for a few days, to visit a friend."

"Oh." I nodded toward the luggage. "Well, thank you for all your help."

"It was nothing." He looked around the room. "Is there anything you need?" He walked over to the bedroom door. "I'll just check that the maid has been here."

I followed him. "I'm sure it's fine. I just left here this morning." He had already crossed the bedroom floor and opened the door to the bathroom. I looked around. The maid had been there. The bed was made, and everything was neat and tidy. The dark furniture made such a nice contrast to the crisp whitewashed walls.

And then I screamed.

Marco spun around and hurried toward me. "What? What is it?"

I raised a trembling finger and pointed at the wall, right above the pillow where I had laid my head last night. On the white wall sat a dark brown scorpion. I stared at it, feeling my heart racing. Scorpions were dangerous! Lethal, even. What was I going to do? We had to get out of here. Call someone, an exterminator or—

Marco just snorted. He turned toward the desk and grabbed the folder with tourist information that lay next to the notepad and complimentary postcards. With a quick flick of the wrist, he opened the window. Then he walked over to the bed, inched the scorpion onto the folder and lifted it outside. After closing the window and putting the folder back in place, he turned toward me. I just stared at him in disbelief. How could he be so cool?

"Thank you," I gasped, still trembling all over from the shock.

He shrugged. "It's no bother."

"B-but ..." I stuttered. "A scorpion?"

Another shrug. "They are quite common around here. They're not dangerous. No worse than a wasp."

I stared at him and then at the wall above my pillow. If I had woken up in the middle of the night and seen that thing staring down at me, my heart would have stopped. Venomous or not, that scorpion would have killed me just by being there.

"Oh god," I whispered and felt my head spin. I was actually feeling pretty faint. "I … Thank you for being here," I said, my voice cracking. "It totally freaked me out, seeing it there, and I don't know what I would have done if you hadn't been here." I glanced over at the window. "But what if it comes back inside?" My heart raced again, and I noticed that my field of vision had narrowed. I was definitely feeling dizzy.

I took one step toward the edge of the bed to sit down but didn't quite make it. Everything went black and I fell.

When I came to a moment later, I was in his arms. Despite the feelings of fear and panic, the most overwhelming emotion of all was the absolute feeling of rightness that came from being pressed to his chest. I couldn't help myself. A small moan of pleasure escaped my lips. Looking up, I saw that he had carried me around to the side of the bed and was bending down to place me on the covers.

"Oh," I gasped. "What happened?"

He put me down and stood up, looking at me with a concerned frown between his dark eyebrows. "You fainted," he said. "Have you eaten this evening?"

I nodded. I had made myself a sandwich before I left, using up the last of the bread.

"Have you been getting enough fluids?" he asked. "It's been very hot today. A lot of tourists forget this."

I tried to sit up. "I'm fine," I protested, but my head was definitely spinning.

"Stay there," he said and disappeared out the door.

Just seeing him leave made me feel as if something tore inside of my chest. I didn't understand. It was just a stupid crush. It wasn't as if I had actual feelings for this man. I didn't know a thing about him. Apart from the fact that he was gorgeous and talented and caring and protective and …

Oh, Heather! Stupid, stupid girl.

He returned just as I was in the middle of admonishing myself for falling for this man. Seeing him made it obvious. My entire body lit up when he came back on through the door.

Oh, no, Heather! Just tell him to leave.

But he had brought me a glass of wine. You don't tell handsome men who bring you yummy wine to go away.

"Thank you," I said breathlessly and took it from him, careful to avoid touching his fingers.

A large gulp did nothing to wash away my feelings. Because that's what they were.

Actual, honest, indisputable feelings.

The only consolation was that they were probably only physical. I was attracted to this handsome man, that was all. My young and viable ovum wanted to be fertilized by his obviously first-class sperm. He would make beautiful and talented babies, of that I was sure, and if I had been in the market for a baby, I wouldn't have thought twice about jumping into bed with Marco, if he'd wanted to.

But I was way too young to have a baby, and Marco had made it painfully obvious that he wasn't attracted to me. I don't know how I could have gotten it so wrong, but I wasn't about to embarrass myself even further.

Marco was definitely off-limits.

I took another sip of the wine and glanced up at the wall. "I don't know how I'll be able to sleep here tonight," I said.

He frowned again. "I can get you another room."

I shook my head. "It might just as easily show up there."

"It will not harm you," he said, and there was some comfort in that. But not as much as there was in his very presence.

I really, really wanted to ask him to stay here with me tonight. But no. I had to be strong.

I got up and walked around the bed, toward the door. "I'll be fine," I said to Marco over my shoulder. I kicked off my shoes as I walked, the first step in getting ready for bed. I don't know if it was the wine on an almost empty stomach, or if it was the strap on my shoe that got hooked on something, but I stumbled and almost fell across the threshold out to the living room.

Once again, Marco was there, catching

me, and this time I was conscious and could enjoy every moment of it. The feeling of his strong arms when he wrapped them around me, hard, was heaven. I groaned out loud and didn't even bother feeling embarrassed about it. This felt so incredibly good! Turning around, I looked up at his face, and what I saw in his eyes changed everything.

It wasn't disgust. Not even a little bit.

It was pure, unadulterated lust.

Oh, Marco.

Oh, no.

10

MARCO

I HAD BEEN RESOLVED to keep my distance as soon as we got out of the car. Getting too close would only get me into trouble. But that little scorpion really frightened her, and I could tell from her pale face that she was upset. When she fainted, I rushed forward to catch her.

It was pure instinct.

Carrying her around to the side of the bed and laying her there where she would be safe and comfortable, I did everything I could to not notice the way she felt in my arms.

Honest to God, I really tried.

But every fiber in my being reacted to her

proximity in a way that quickly spiraled out of control. The feeling of her in my arms … the scent of her in my nostrils … the sound of her moan that sounded so much like a cry of passion that it took all my self-restraint to back away from the bed.

She was a vision, lying there, pale and trembling, her eyes wide and her lips parted.

So beautiful. So vulnerable.

I had to get away from here.

Fetching her a glass of wine got me out of the bedroom at least, and then I waited a few steps back from the bed while she drank. I just wanted to see some color return to those pale cheeks before I dared to leave her alone, but after only a couple of sips she insisted that she was fine and got up, even though it was obvious that she wasn't.

That stupid girl. So reckless.

As soon as she started to move toward the door, I knew it was going to end badly. She tried to remove her shoes as she was walking, but she was looking back at me and something went wrong.

The surprised look on her face when her foot caught on something and she fell …

I had promised myself that I would never touch her again, never even get near, but what was I going to do?

I couldn't just let her fall, surely?

Wrapping my arms around her to keep her from harm felt like the most natural thing to do, but at the same time, I could feel all my carefully tethered impulses tugging at their restraints.

Holding her close felt so … right. So good. So very, very … arousing.

I turned her over and she lifted her face up toward me, staring into my eyes. Her lips parted and she gasped at what she must have seen in mine.

Did I scare you, darling girl?

I felt like the big bad wolf, drooling over that innocent young girl, and a small, sensible part of my brain knew that I needed to just help her to her feet and then get the hell out of that suite before something terrible happened.

The larger part of my brain, on the other hand, was focused on her soft, red lips, wondering what they might taste like.

I knew it was wrong. I knew it.

But I couldn't help myself. Staring into her eyes, I bent forward and stole a kiss.

It was a stupid thing to do, don't get me wrong. I knew that. There was no rhyme or reason behind my actions. It was pure instinct.

It was only ever going to be that one brief kiss. I expected her to push me away, to object, to bite my lip, to scream.

Anything.

Anything but what actually happened.

La bella signorina Americana kissed me back. Eagerly.

Her hand slid around the back of my neck and pulled me closer, until our lips crushed against one another in a way that was almost more painful than pleasurable.

The words *This is wrong!* kept going through my mind, but it was too late. I had crossed a line and now there was no turning back. I plunged headfirst into that kiss, tasting, sucking, nibbling, exploring, and there was no stopping me now. My hands moved over her body, completely without abandon, not even caring anymore about how wrong this was.

Who cared about right or wrong in a moment like this?

Why didn't she tell me to stop? I don't know that I would have been able to, but still …

Oh, Giulietta, I'm so sorry, I thought, and I felt tears stinging at the back of my eyes as I found the small buttons of her dress and undid them, one by one, revealing a black lace bra stuffed with the most amazing breasts I'd ever seen. I wanted to fall to my knees and worship them, that would have been the only right thing to do, but instead, I picked her up and carried her back into the bedroom.

We landed on the bed with a crash that I barely heard for the thudding of my heartbeats in my eardrums. The beast had been unleashed and there was no stopping it now. I had to do this. I had to claim this beautiful girl and take all that she had to offer me.

There was no other way this night was going to end.

I hated myself for it, and I would never be able to forgive myself, but … it couldn't be helped.

I could not see any other way out of this, other than me burying myself deep inside of this beautiful creature's miraculous body.

There were so many fiddly buttons getting in the way, too many. I may have torn her dress in my desperation. I hope not. But before long, there she was, lying completely naked on the bedspread. She was trembling, but I don't think it was from the cold. Her eyes were wide, but she stared straight into mine without the slightest fear. As if she wanted this. As if she … longed for it?

That didn't seem real, but this was not the time to question a blessing such as this.

I climbed on top of her and she spread her soft thighs wide. It was unreal, surreal, out of this world, and I didn't know how to deal with all the emotions that swelled up from my repressed depths.

I did the only thing I could, and plunged deep inside of her, in search of something I didn't feel that I deserved.

11

HEATHER

HE TORE at my clothes but didn't seem to make enough progress, so I had to help him out. There was something wild and almost sad in his eyes, but I was feeling pretty wild myself right now, and if there was anything I could do to ease his sadness, I would be only too happy to.

Laying there naked on the bed, looking up at him as he stood over me, I felt something resembling relief come over me. There had been this tension between us since he first carried me from my car, through the nettles, and I hadn't been able to figure out what it meant, but now all the pieces were falling into place.

This felt so right. I wanted him and he wanted me, and we were going to give each other comfort and pleasures, of that I was sure. This was going to be intense.

Spreading my legs as far as they would go, I stared up at him, urging him on with unspoken signals. There was no need to hold back. I was ready. More than ready.

As he slowly inched inside of me, I looked him in the eyes, and there was a connection there that I had never experienced before. It made it all so much more intense, every movement so much more palpable.

He pushed himself as deep as he could go, and then he stopped. I wrapped my legs around him, holding him in place. Lifting one hand to cup his cheek, I looked deep into his eyes and smiled in a way that I hoped would reassure him. He seemed worried. Worried and sad. What was he afraid of? That I would expect something from him if we did this? That was usually what scared boys off. Fear of commitment.

"It's OK," I whispered. "Don't think. Just feel." I caressed his cheek. "Doesn't that feel good? Hm?"

He looked pained for a moment, but then he nodded slowly.

"Good," I whispered. "That's all this needs to be. Two people making each other feel good."

He was holding himself up above me, and apart from being joined at the hip so to speak, we were barely touching. I let my hand slide down from his face, along his neck and onto his chest. A sparse mat of black hairs covered it. The hairs felt soft underneath my palm. Still, he didn't speak.

I continued to speak, my voice still not much more than a whisper. "What can I do to make you feel good?"

His eyes only left my face for a moment, but I could tell where they went. It was no surprise. The girls were my best features, by far. All the boys thought so.

Loosening the grip my thighs had around his hips, I pushed him to the side so that we could roll over and switch places, careful not to let him slip out. It felt so great to feel him there, deep inside of me. So intimate. So … close.

With me on top, he had a great view of

the girls, and I could see his eyes widen as he tried to take them all in. I leaned forward and moved slowly from side to side, hypnotizing him with my nipples. Deep within me, I could feel him growing even larger, even harder. My nipples were stiff and protruding and I let them move past his mouth, just close enough that they brushed against his lips. On the second or third pass, he managed to latch on, and sucked the nipple hard to stop me from moving away. I could feel the suction deep inside of my core and wished that I could suck his cock inside of me in the same way. We lay there, almost completely still, him sucking my breast, me clenching my internal muscles around his solid shaft. After what felt like an eternity, he slowly let go. I brushed my glistening nipple across his cheek and then let him have the other one. The look in his eyes was primal. Eventually, he seemed to relax, and he started easing up, alternating the intense sucking with licking and kisses, around the nipples and into the cleft between my breasts. He had to use both hands to hold them and seemed in awe of their heft. Yeah, I had a lot to offer a man, and it seemed I had finally found a man who knew to appreciate it all. He looked almost reverent in the way he handled them.

Don't get me wrong. I had no problem with being an object of worship. Especially not when it felt so damn good with his intense licking and kissing and tracing patterns with his tongue. I couldn't stay still any longer, so I started to move back and forth, feeling his thick shaft sliding out a bit and then back in again. Grinding my clit against his pelvic bone, I got just the right amount of friction that I needed and was starting to feel myself soar when he suddenly seemed to realize that there was more to me than just my breasts.

We switched places again, but this time, he was on his knees leaning forward, holding my hips aloft with one strong hand. The other hand found my swollen clit and rubbed it at just the right intensity while he started to thrust. With my hips suspended like that, I didn't get any traction, so I just lay back and enjoyed the ride. It was glorious, his thick cock filling me up completely with every push forward and his skilled fingers creating the perfect recipe for a magnificent orgasm. I was grateful that there were no neighbors out here because I could hear my moans escalate into screams that rose in intensity every time he pushed himself inside of me. He fit so perfectly; it was as if we were made for each other.

Just as I was about to reach the peak, he stopped. I opened my eyes and saw him staring down at me. The admiration or perhaps even adoration in his eyes was obvious. As eager as I was to reach that orgasm, I smiled at him. Then I pushed him away, just enough so that I could roll over and get up on all fours. Presenting him with my naked backside, I looked over my shoulder and gave him an encouraging nod. He didn't need to be asked twice. His strong hands grabbed my hips hard and then his cock pushed as deep inside of me as it could go. I braced myself with one hand while the other rubbed my clit, but I really didn't need to. The feeling of him ramming hard against my butt and his cock reaching places inside of me that no one had ever reached was enough to

drive me to orgasm within a couple of minutes. I screamed and pushed my hips back to
meet his last couple of thrusts, even though I
was completely spent. Marco followed me
into the bliss just a moment or two later and
we collapsed on the bed, completely en-
tangled.

MARCO

FOR THE FIRST time in a decade, I slept through the night. If I had any dreams, they weren't about Giulietta. During the first moments after waking the next morning, I didn't even remember to feel bad about it.

I awoke in the garden suite, *la bella signorina Americana* snuggled up against me. Her dark hair was tousled and covered most of her face. I eased it to the side, careful not to wake her. Her body was warm and soft and seemed to have molded around my shape in a way that felt like destiny.

But I didn't believe in destiny.

At least not a destiny that meant that I got

to wake up in the arms of such an amazing woman every morning.

I shifted slightly, and she rolled over with a dreaming sigh, letting go of me. The room was warm, but the absence of her made my skin feel cold and deprived.

Less than a minute since we parted, and I was already missing her.

Inching out of bed, I searched for my clothes that were spread out around the room, slipping them on. While I moved through the room, my eyes kept finding her shape underneath the sheets, and I couldn't help but compare her to Giulietta as the guilt of what I had done crashed down on me like a ton of bricks.

This girl was so young; her face completely smooth apart from a couple of creases where her cheek had pressed against the wrinkled pillowcase. Giulietta had been my age, so about to turn 34 when … I pressed my eyes shut hard to keep the images from my retina. This girl was blessed with divine curves that would drive any man insane. Giulietta had been slim, with perky little breasts that hadn't even needed a bra.

They had never come crashing down on me in bed, like this girl's amazing breasts had done last night. I had thought that I had died and gone to heaven, and just thinking about it now made me hard. This girl was an artist, and Giulietta had worked in administration at the local council, all computers and spreadsheets. This girl was an American, Giulietta had been undeniably Italian. This girl was short, Giulietta had been almost as tall as me.

The two women couldn't be more different. And I had loved Giulietta passionately, convinced that there would never be anyone but her for me.

And now, it felt as if I had betrayed her.

If it had just been the sex, I think I could have pushed through the guilt. Perhaps Giulietta would have understood that a man has needs, and ten years is a long time for a man in his prime to go celibate.

But looking down at the sleeping young woman, I felt a dawning realization creep up my spine like some creature from the darkness come to claim my soul. This, what had happened here, hadn't been just about sex.

If it had, I could have just walked out this door, spent and satisfied, and never looked back. Perhaps I could even have made a habit out of it, of jumping into bed with female guests, once every ten years or so, just to release some of the pent-up frustrations of my solitary existence.

But no. That wasn't the future I was picturing for myself, not at all, as I stood here at the foot of the bed, looking down at *la bella signorina*. Instead, my head was filled with images of the two of us, together. Not just naked in bed, like last night. But in life.

And that, I knew, was too much of a betrayal of Giulietta for me to be able to bear.

I had promised her to be true. I had sworn to never look at another woman, and those promises from our wedding day felt as binding this morning as they had done when I spoke them out loud all those years ago.

Looking down at the sleeping beauty in the bed before me, I came to a painful realization.

I was never going to be able to leave my past behind me.

This magnificent young woman deserved a man who didn't come with a past like mine.

She deserved a man who could be all hers.

Leaving the garden suite, I closed the door behind me, careful not to wake her. Sure, it was a cowardly move, sneaking off at dawn without even leaving a note. But it was for the best, or at least that's what I kept telling myself.

If I had stayed until she woke, I might never have been able to leave.

13

HEATHER

I SLEPT, and in my dreams, I was enveloped by strong arms. I couldn't see his face, but I knew it was him. And I knew it was right.

It was stupid really, because the only thing I'd been after this summer had been a hot Italian fling. I hadn't been looking for Mr. Right, only *signor* Right Now. Perhaps even a couple of different *signores*. I was too young to want to settle down with just the one guy, and when I did, I certainly planned on doing it back home, not in some faraway country where I didn't know a single soul.

No man was worth giving up my friends.

The warm embrace slipped away, and I turned, searching for it. Suddenly the soft light that had surrounded me melted away, and everything went dark. In my dream, I walked down a long corridor, opening doors to the left and right. I didn't know what I was looking for, but it didn't matter, because all the rooms were empty.

At the end of the corridor, I could just make out a dim light, and as I stared at it, something moved across it, a tall silhouette moving from left to right. The spark of joy in my heart when I saw him told me everything I needed to know.

He was the one.

I started running down the corridor, ignoring all the doors, even those that stood ajar. But the corridor was long and as fast as I ran, I didn't seem to get any closer. The tall silhouette moved away, into the shadows, and disappeared from sight.

I think I cried out, a helpless plea or maybe his name, but perhaps that was just in the dream.

When I woke up, I was tangled in the sheets. My heart was racing, and I sat up, looking around the room, confused and bewildered. Where did he go? In my mind's eye, I saw the shape of him move past the light at the end of the corridor. Even if he had been far away, I knew that it was him. Marco.

He had been here, hadn't he? Or was that just a dream as well?

But the state of the bed, and my clothes that lay scattered around the room, reassured me. I hadn't just dreamed our night together. It had been real. Oh, so real.

Oh, Heather!

Slipping out of bed, I found the bathrobe and walked out into the other room.

"Marco?"

But the living room was empty, and there was no sign of him. I walked back into the bedroom and checked the nightstands and the desk. No note. Nothing.

Rubbing my face to try and rid myself of the sleepy confusion, I sat down on the edge of the bed. My bra was hanging across the back of the desk chair. I couldn't remember taking it off, but other memories of last night came flooding back like a tidal wave, and I felt the emotions hit me hard.

As distanced and polite as Marco had

been, there was no denying the intensity of our coupling, or the emotions in his eyes right before he kissed me for the first time. He had feelings for me, but were those feelings strictly physical?

The restless longing that drove me to wander from room to room, looking for signs of him, told me that whatever *I* was feeling was something above and beyond what we had done together last night. As glorious and intensely satisfying as that had been.

But what did it mean that he had left before I woke up? Surely, if this had been something more than just a one-night stand, he would have stayed? And if something had forced him to leave, a work thing, for instance, he would have left a note? I checked the desk again, but the pad with the *monasterio's* letterhead on was blank.

Maybe I had misinterpreted what I'd seen. Perhaps I had fallen prey to the old wishful thinking fallacy.

I had wanted him to want me, on more than just the physical level, and so I had interpreted his desire as something more.

Oh, stupid Heather, I admonished myself. You don't *want* him to fall in love with you. It was just sex. Great sex. He needed something, and you needed something, and you helped each other out, and it was great.

End of story.

But as I wandered out into the other room again and took a handful of grapes from *signora* Balducci's fruit basket, I felt the clear and sharp pain of abandonment that I had felt enough times in my life to recognize.

Even in Italian.

14

MARCO

THE CAR still smelled faintly of fish as I drove down the winding road on my way toward the coast. I only had the faintest idea of where I was going, but I knew that I had to get away.

There was no way I could stay in the *monasterio* this week. Not with *la bella signorina* Heather staying in the garden suite.

Not now that I'd had a taste of what she had to offer.

I still couldn't quite wrap my mind around what had happened between us, what we had done, what I had done to her, and I had to constantly push the memorable images from my mind. I couldn't think about that; I mustn't ever think about that.

Never again.

There was only one solution. I had to get away. I had to get as far away from that temptation as I could get and stay away until I knew for certain that *signorina* Heather had left.

I could never be in the same room as her again.

Not now that I knew what she felt like. What she could wake in me.

The guilt and shame felt like molten iron against my skin, and tears stung at the back of my eyes.

I'm so sorry, Giulietta, I pleaded wordlessly. *I didn't mean for it to happen. You know that I could never love another woman. It was just … sex.*

But unlike all the other times I had spoken to Giulietta in my mind, this time she didn't reply. I couldn't even picture her face, other than a dim view of her turning away from me.

I couldn't even convince myself of the truth in that statement.

If it had been just sex, then why did I have to leave?

I gritted my teeth and clenched my fists around the steering wheel. There was a logic in that statement that made me feel sick. I spotted a lay-by up ahead and switched on the indicator, pulling off the road.

Sitting in the car, parked under a tree for some well-needed shade, I stared ahead, not seeing anything of the surroundings. All I could see was *signorina* Heather, straddling me, leaning forward and offering me her glorious breasts. Heather, standing on all four in front of me, looking back over one shoulder, her eyes glazed over by the imminent orgasm.

Rubbing my hands over my face, I groaned out loud.

It *had* been just about the sex, I told myself. Of course, it had been. And the sex had been great. That was why it felt so wrong, driving away from the *monasterio*.

Because la bella signorina *Heather is going to be there all week, and just think about all the great sex you could be having during her stay in the garden suite.*

Picturing more nights together in her bed made me feel faint, but also aroused. There was so much more we could do. So much more we could experience.

And after a week, I would be satisfied, surely. I would be well and truly spent. I would be able to return to my monastic existence, just working and slaving away to pay the bills and keep the business going.

After ten years of hard work, didn't I deserve a break? Didn't I deserve to let off some steam?

As long as it was just about the sex, could you forgive me, Giulietta?

I searched my mind for her face, searched my soul for her answer. But all I got was silence.

I started the car and drove up to the exit, looking up and down the road. What should I do? If I continued toward the coast, wouldn't that be the same as admitting that I had feelings for *signorina* Heather? And wouldn't that be worse than just having sex with her?

It's been ten years, a voice at the back of my mind said. *Maybe it's time you let her go ...*

I shook my head violently. No. Never. Giulietta was my one true love. There would never be another woman in my life, could never be.

But then … that ought to mean that I could have some fun with the young American.

If what was going on between us was purely physical.

I stared up and down the road. Toward the coast. Back toward the *monasterio*. Love. Or sex. Betrayal. Or … what? Giulietta or Heather?

No. NO!

That was *not* what this was about. Heather could never replace Giulietta. She was half her age. She was a stranger. A tourist.

She meant nothing to me.

Giulietta meant everything.

Well then, said the voice at the back of my mind. *If you're certain that* la bella signorina Americana *doesn't pose a threat to what you had with Giulietta …*

And then my mind was filled with images of Heather, naked in the bed in the garden suite. Memories ... and enticing thoughts about things we hadn't even tried yet.

Looking up the road toward the coast once more, I cursed. And then I turned the car back toward the *monasterio*.

15

HEATHER

I WON'T DENY IT; I felt a bit tousled, emotionally, as I set up my easel in the garden. There had been no sign of Marco at breakfast either, and I hadn't dared to ask any of the staff for him.

I didn't want to come off as clingy.

And he might not want anyone to know what had happened between us.

Pushing the memories from my mind, I tried to focus on my work. This was what I was here for. Not for some guy. It was yet another sunny morning, and I wanted to get as much work done as possible before the mid-day heat forced me indoors.

Selecting my colors and squeezing them

out onto my small palette, I looked around at all the magnificent sights, trying to decide on what should be my five motifs.

Was it really just yesterday morning that I had stood in this exact same spot, sketching like mad? Inspired as I had never been before?

And now?

With a sigh, I lowered my palette and stared at the blank easel.

All I could think about was him. And us. Together.

Damn it, Heather!

I wanted to scream. Cry. Bang my head against something hard, like that brick wall over there. Why did I always do this? As soon as some guy showed me an ounce of affection, I fell like a ton of bricks. This was just supposed to be a holiday fling.

Focus on the work at hand, Heather!

But staring at the blank canvas, I didn't see any of the beautiful views that surrounded me. All I saw was him. His hands. His chest. His lips on my breasts.

Putting my palette down on the grass, I picked up some charcoal and did a quick sketch. Just his face and torso, turned half away from me, just like in my dream.

Using my fingers, I smudged in some shadows, blurred some lines to create dimension. And slowly he appeared.

Staring at his glowing eyes on the canvas before me, I placed a hand gently on his chest. Blinking the tears from my eyes, I came to a decision.

I had *not* come to Italy for some guy. I had come here for my work. To learn and grow as a painter, as an artist. Grandpa hadn't left me that money so that I could go gallivanting around with men. He had wanted me to work on my craft.

Live and love, with no regrets ...

Gritting my teeth, I dropped the charcoal in my painter's box and loosened the screws that held the canvas in place. That was easier said than done, Grandpa, I muttered. Love always led to regrets, as far as I was concerned.

AS THE SUN began to set across the valley, I

wiped off my brushes and started to pack up. It had been a long day, and I was beat, both physically and creatively.

How about emotionally? some prying voice at the back of my mind inquired, but I shook my head and looked at my canvases that stood lined up along the inside of the garden wall. There were seven of them, and none of them were finished, but I think that I had managed to find a fine selection of motifs. It was important that they all worked together, as a collection, and that they should all work as marketing material for the *monasterio*.

I couldn't imagine that it was difficult to market a place like this, though. It was pure magic, and too beautiful for words. The fact that there were so few guests staying here had to be a deliberate choice on *signora* Balducci's part, to create a sense of exclusivity.

I had to go back and forth several times before I had moved all my paintings and supplies into the garden suite, and by the time I was done, I was beat. A shower, and then straight to bed. There was no way I could manage a four-course dinner in the formal dining room after the day I'd had.

And I also wasn't sure how I'd feel about running into Marco.

The fact that he had left without so much as a note this morning, and then stayed away all day, even though he knew exactly where I was, told me that he considered our night together to be a mistake, or at least not something that should be repeated. And I won't deny it. That hurt!

Ignoring the fact that my heart seemed set on him being the one, as if this was some kind of fairytale, last night had been great. Not just for me. I was sure of that. But no matter how great it had been, I wasn't going to go begging for more.

With a sigh, I peeled off my sweaty clothes and stepped into the shower. Being out in the sun all day had made my skin tender, even though I had used plenty of sunblock and tried to stay in the shade. I turned the tap over toward the blue dot and let the cool water soothe my skin. Running my hands over my body, my mind was once again flooded with memories of last night, and I pushed my face into the flow of water to wash away the stinging tears.

It had felt so good, so right, but it had been a one-time thing, apparently. I would have to make do with the memories.

After the shower, I almost collapsed on the bed, but forced myself to go into the other room and find something to eat. This time around, the refrigerator was stocked with little treats, but I just snagged some chocolate and a glass of wine from a large box on the top shelf, too tired to even cut some cheese and bread.

Sipping the overly chilled wine and nibbling the dark chocolate, I stood surveying my paintings that were arranged on every available surface. *Focus on the work, Heather,* I admonished myself. This you have some control over, unlike some Italian chef that you can barely stop thinking of.

I made myself walk from canvas to canvas and consider the choices I had made so far, angles, perspectives, color choices, planning the next step, and so on. Just as I was starting to get absorbed into the work for real, there was a knock on the door.

I almost jumped out of my skin, and for several seconds, I just stood there, staring at it. Then I pulled myself together, tightened the belt on my bathrobe and walked over to the door.

Outside stood a young woman dressed as a waiter.

"Good evening, *signorina*," she said, smiling politely. "Chef asked me to find out if you were joining us in the dining room this evening, or if you would like to have dinner served in your suite?"

I stared at her. "Er …"

'Chef' had asked her? Meaning, Marco had asked her? Was this some kind of code? Was he playing some kind of game? I shook my head. "Thank you, but I'll be skipping dinner tonight," I said, trying to keep the hurt out of my voice. I don't think I was very successful at it.

She kept smiling, and I couldn't help wondering if she knew what had happened. Was this something 'Chef' always did? Served dessert with a little something on the side to all the *signorinas* who stayed at the hotel? I felt my cheeks start to heat up and began to close the door. This was humiliating.

"Very well, *signorina*. I wish you a good

night," she said, and disappeared back into the shadows.

I slammed the door shut and went and refilled my glass. To bed, alone, and hopefully, sleep would come quickly.

It was going to be another long day of work tomorrow.

16

MARCO

THE KITCHEN WAS hot and steamy, and I was aching all over from lack of sleep, lack of rest and … something else that I was lacking. Luca dropped a saucepan with a clang against the flagstone floor and I didn't even have the energy to rant at him for making a mess. Instead, I just frowned at him, wiped my forehead with a towel, and turned back to the stove. I could easily picture the looks the boys gave each other behind my back, but today, I didn't care about any of that. I had other things on my mind.

Not even the fragrances that rose from my pots and pans could soothe the chafing that I had walked around with all day.

Even though I had made some kind of decision there at the lay-by, I still hadn't been able to go to *signorina* Heather when I got back to the *monasterio*. I had returned to my rooms to get changed for work, and had stood for a long while at my window, looking down at the garden.

Looking down at her.

She had been out there most of the day, hard at work. I had to admire the way she took on the impossible task my mother had given her. Mama would surely be pleased with the finished artwork.

But I was certain that no postcards would be able to turn this place around. The *monasterio* had been in the red for as long as I could remember, and not even all the hard work that I had put into it over the past ten years had been able to turn things around.

We were going to need a miracle of some sort, or the *monasterio* would be out of business by the end of the year.

But there was no way I was going to get through the last months here if I thought about that.

Anna came back from the garden suite

and I glanced at her. She shook her head. I raised my eyebrows.

"Nothing for the garden suite tonight, Chef," she said, and picked up the plates that Luca had finished. "Sorry," she added and carried them toward the door.

I turned back to my pans, feeling the heat from the gas burners against my face. Surely, that heat was the only reason my face felt hot. Surely, my staff couldn't read my mind. They didn't know what was going on.

They couldn't.

I mean, I barely knew myself.

EVENING SERVICE WAS SWIFT, all happy customers and praise from the dining room, but I wasn't listening to what Anna said when she returned with the empty plates. I was busy prepping tomorrow night's dinner, intensely focused on the task at hand so that I wouldn't have time to think about why *signorina* Heather hadn't come in for dinner.

She must be tired, of course. But then, why hadn't she ordered room service?

I stopped, a sprig of rosemary in my hand, and stared into space. I had expected her to ask for dinner served in her suite. After all, she must be as tired as I was, after the day she'd had. And I had thought that … after I had served her dinner, we could have picked up where we left off last night.

Signorina Heather didn't look like a woman who didn't care about dinner. She had clearly enjoyed the food I had served her last night. So it couldn't have been the food that she had turned down.

It must have been me.

With a frustrated groan, I covered the platter with cling film and slid it into the re-frigerator.

It was clear that the lovely *signorina* had no desire to continue our explorations from last night.

Tearing the sweaty bandana from my head, I took one last look around the kitchen to make sure that everything was as it should be.

And then I went upstairs to bed.

Alone.

17

HEATHER

I SLEPT like the dead and woke early, feeling a little bit more like my old self.

See, I told myself. Time heals all wounds. I'll get over this. It will all be a sweet memory by the end of the summer. A memory that I'll treasure when I get back home.

But home felt so remote as I moved my things out into the garden and got started. Once again, I focused on the work, and let the creation of these paintings take over. Slowly but surely, the motifs I'd chosen started to take shape, even though there was still much work to be done. *Signora* Balducci would be pleased with my work, even if her son might wish I'd never come back.

My second day back at the *monasterio* was much like the first. All work, some light snacks from my own stash, and then early to bed. Thankfully I was too tired from working all day to even worry about scorpions or handsome men whose touch drove me wild, and I was asleep almost as soon as my head hit the pillow.

WHEN I WOKE up on the third day, there was something different about the light in the bedroom. I glanced over at the window. I'd left the curtains open to wake up with the sun, but the light that came in was dull and gray. Crawling out of bed, I made my way over to the window and peered out. The sky was overcast, and it looked as if it might rain later.

Walking into the living room, I took a good look at my paintings and decided not to let a day without sun disparage me. I had made great progress, and even if I did nothing at all today, I'd still finish *signora* Balducci's paintings before the deadline she'd set. And I would be able to work on a couple of the paintings here in my suite, the ones where I had found the right color palette, and I just needed to apply the paints.

I reached my arms over my head and stretched like a cat, trying to force the sleepy stiffness from my joints. Well, if I was going to work all day, I deserved a proper breakfast.

Once I had showered and gotten dressed, I made my way through the garden and back inside the main building. A few drops hit me on the way, but it hadn't started to rain properly yet. The breakfast room was almost empty. It was still early, and I guessed that the other guests had chosen to postpone their sightseeing plans and sleep in. The buffet table was as laden as usual with delicious breakfast foods and I filled my plate with a little bit of everything.

By the time I had finished my breakfast, the rain was pouring down. The water flowed down the large windows and the room had gone almost entirely dark. I put my plate and coffee mug away and walked toward the door, but the thought of venturing outside in the downpour made me turn in the other direction. I might as well explore the rest of the building while I waited for the rain to abate.

The reception was empty, and the sign on the desk said to ring the bell for assistance. I wasn't in need of any particular assistance, so I just kept walking and found another corridor on the other side. At the end of it was a large stained-glass window that I decided to take a closer look at. It wasn't as impressive in the glum gray light as I'm sure it would have been in the usual sunlight, but it was still stunning. I stood for a long time just looking at the faces of the saints depicted, trying to figure out how the artist had managed to capture the look of suffering while still making them look so beautiful. Especially one man on the far left of the window caught my eye. There was something about him that reminded me of Marco. The sadness in his eyes. The closed-off posture. All the invisible walls he had erected around himself.

Don't flatter yourself, the voice at the back of my head said. *He's just not into you.*

But I wasn't sure that it was true. There was pain there, and it had been there from the start, from the very first moment I saw him.

I hadn't caused that pain.

But I wouldn't mind a chance to soothe it …

18

MARCO

I WOKE to the sound of rain pelting my windows. There was a chill in the air that I welcomed, even though goosebumps spread across my naked skin as I rolled over and pushed the sheets off me. For a long time I just lay there, staring at the ceiling, trying to shake off the weird sensations that had followed me from my dream state into the glum daylight. I couldn't remember what the dream had been about, but it had been intense. Even though I had just woken up, I felt weary and my whole body tingled, as if I'd run a marathon.

Rubbing my face with both hands, I groaned. I couldn't remember anything about the dream—apart from the fact that *she* had been in it. I pushed myself up onto the side of the bed, scratching my scalp. It had been 48 hours since I walked away from *signorina* Heather, asleep in the garden suite, and as much as I had tried to forget, she had never left my mind, whether awake or asleep.

What happened to getting all these tensions out of your system? the nasty voice at the back of my head said. *Weren't you supposed to spend these few nights with her, blowing off steam, huh?*

Staggering to my feet, I moved across the icy floor toward the window. The rain came down so hard I could barely make out any part of the stunning view. Yeah, perhaps that had been the plan when I sat there at the lay-by, but in the end, I hadn't been able to go to her.

And she hadn't come to me, and that proved that my decision had been the right one. It had just been a one-time thing for her, and she wasn't interested in a repeat.

Who could blame her? A young, beautiful, talented woman like her. And an old, bitter, broken man like me.

It could never work.

Fragments of my dreams bubbled up in my mind, and they all seemed to contradict that statement. I couldn't make any sense of them, but they all seemed to portray me and that wonderful young woman together in different scenarios, not all of them in a state of undress.

Together. And happy.

Shaking my head, I pushed away from the glass and went to get dressed.

Me happy?

What a ridiculous concept!

19

HEATHER

Turning away from the stained-glass window, I made my way back the long corridor. The rain showed no sign of letting up, so I was in no rush. One of the doors I walked past was open, and just like in some of the rooms I had seen when I first arrived, it had some impressive murals. The room was completely empty, not even any furniture, so I ventured inside to take a closer look.

It was a vast space, almost like a ballroom, with the flagstone floor worn smooth by several hundred years of footsteps. Even in the glum light, it was a beautiful and inspiring space. Perhaps I could paint in here this afternoon if the rain persisted.

Walking over to the middle of the room, I stood for a long time studying the mural that covered the entire wall from floor to ceiling. It was humbling to think of the artists that had stood right here where I was standing now and pictured the scenery in the painting before getting to work. I wondered if they had thought about their work being seen by people many hundred years into the future.

I thought about my own paintings being made into postcards and perhaps pillows and smiled ruefully. Yeah, not quite on the same level as these guys …

I made my way back, and when I came to the reception, the woman was standing behind the counter.

"*Buona sera, signorina,*" she said and smiled.

"Good morning," I replied. "I was wondering," I gestured over my shoulder, "that large hall at the end of the corridor … would it be okay if I painted in there today, if the rain continues?"

She peered behind me. "Of course. No one ever uses that room." She waved dismissively with one well-manicured hand. "Go ahead."

I frowned. "I'll make sure to cover the floor," I said. "You don't want to get any paint on those lovely stones."

She shook her head. "As I said, it's not a room that we ever use for anything. Don't bother."

I looked back down the corridor. "Really? I would have thought that a room like that would be perfect for weddings or large parties."

The receptionist just smiled. "No, we don't do weddings. No parties. Only Agriturismo."

I thought that was a bit strange but thanked her and made my way back to the door out toward the garden. The rain showed no sign of holding up, and I stood for a while peering out into the semi-darkness, debating whether I should run for it. I would get soaked. But then, I was missing out on valuable work time.

A door opened somewhere behind me and I glanced over my shoulder.

It was him.

Marco had stepped out through a door halfway down the corridor, buttoning the last buttons on his chef's jacket as he kicked the door shut behind him. He was turned more or less away from me, exactly like in my dream, and I felt a jolt in my chest just from seeing that semi-profile.

I had managed to get through two whole days without seeing him, but that didn't mean that his effect on me had abated, not in the least.

Oh, Heather!

Something made him turn his head toward me, and as soon as he spotted me, he froze, both hands on his collar. For a moment that felt like a lifetime, we stood there, just looking at each other.

He finally got the last of the buttons closed and let his hands drop. He took a couple of steps toward me, but then he stopped.

"*Signorina* Heather," he said quietly.

"Marco," I replied.

I had no idea what to do. The last time we met, we had come so close, and now, here we stood as complete strangers, separated by a few feet and a massive chunk of awkwardness.

"I didn't know you started work this early," I said, trying to sound casual and cheerful. "The *monasterio* doesn't serve lunch, so …"

He nodded slowly but didn't reply.

I gestured toward the open doorway behind me. "It's raining," I said, feeling like an idiot.

He nodded again. "Can you paint in your suite?"

"I could," I acknowledged. "But the receptionist said I could work in the grand hall. The light is better there."

He glanced over his shoulder with a small frown. Then he nodded. "Elana said that? Yes, we never use it. Go ahead."

"Thank you," I mumbled. This was so awkward; it made my skin crawl. Standing here playing at being polite strangers, when all I wanted was to run into his arms and kiss him … It was no easy feat.

I looked behind me at the rain, coming down hard on the pretty garden. Getting soaked would be a lot less uncomfortable than this.

"Well, I should—" I said, nodding toward the door, at the same time as he said, "I was just going to—" and pointed in the other direction.

"Sorry," we both said at the same time. I blushed and hated my face for being so obvious.

Gritting my teeth, I took one step toward him. "Listen, Marco …" I forced myself to look him in the eyes, his sad, beautiful eyes … Whatever had made him so sad, I hadn't managed to wipe it from his face. "About what happened …"

I ran out of courage when I saw the smoldering fire in his eyes. The intense longing that had made me kiss him the first time. It ignited something inside of me that I quickly stomped out.

"I'm sorry I left without saying goodbye," he said softly.

"Yeah? Then, why did you?" I pushed my hair from my face and looked up at him from under my lashes. He was too handsome for me to look straight at him.

He took another step toward me. "That's not important," he said. "What matters is that I wanted to come back."

Little flames of longing burst up inside of my chest. "You did?"

He nodded. "I just didn't know … I didn't think that …" He shook his head slightly. "That you would want me to."

I sighed deeply and blinked the tears from my eyes. Had I not wanted him to? Only with every fiber of my being. Only every minute of every day and every night. It was pathetic, really. And also, absolutely and deliciously wonderful.

I was only here for a few short days, and then I would never see him again. Why not forget about all the reasons why this would be a bad idea, and just … fall into this man's arms and take whatever he wanted to give me.

"I would want you to," I said, my voice so weak that it was barely audible over the thundering rain. "I would want you to, very much."

There was a faint shadow of a smile on his lips, but he nodded. I was blown away by the seriousness of his expression, even at a time like this. A girl might be deceived into thinking that he wasn't a very passionate man, but I knew better. It took every ounce of my self-control not to throw myself at him, right then and there.

I gathered my wits and tossed my hair over my shoulder. "You're working," I said, gesturing to his prim chef's outfit. "And I also need to get back to work. But perhaps we could … get together later?"

The faint smile turned into a grimace. "I'll be working late."

I felt a tingle at the idea of him showing up with dessert once again. "That's fine," I said quietly. "Bring me a treat."

The heat in his eyes nearly scorched me, and before I made a fool of myself, I turned and walked out the door. Not even the torrential downpour managed to put out the flames he'd lit within me.

20

MARCO

Dinner service was finished almost twenty minutes ago, but I couldn't seem to tear myself away from the kitchen. I had sent the others home and busied myself with straightening things that were already straight, wiping down already clean surfaces.

What was it that was holding me back? I couldn't figure it out. My emotions were all over the place, and I had been acting out of character all evening.

She was waiting for me in the garden suite, so why was I still here? This wasn't rocket science; there was nothing I needed to figure out.

I should just go to her. Do the things we

were bound to do if we found ourselves alone together again.

There was nothing complicated about that. It had all been so seamlessly uncomplicated the first time.

And it was purely physical, so why was my emotions getting all tangled up in a tight knot?

Putting the towel down, I stared at my dim reflection in the stainless-steel backdrop above the range. It was warped and lacked a clear outline, and I thought that I had never seen myself as clearly as that before.

Just go to her, the nasty voice at the back of my head complained. *She's only here for a couple more nights. You've missed out on so much already.*

The constant loop of memories and fantasies had been running non-stop through my mind since I'd left her and created a state of pent-up tension that would have to find some relief soon.

Or else?

Or I might spontaneously combust, probably.

With a sigh, I tore off the bandana that I

wore to keep the grease and food scents out of my hair and threw it in the laundry bin by the door. Fetching a small tray from one of the large refrigerators, I left the kitchen. The garden was still and empty and I crossed it in just a few long strides. Knocking on her door, I checked my watch and noticed the time.

Was I too late? *Signorina* Heather woke up early to paint; I knew that. How selfish of me to keep her waiting.

But before I could change my mind, the door opened and there she was.

It was apparent that she hadn't gone to bed. She was still dressed, and she had three paintbrushes in one hand and a streak of yellow paint along one cheek.

"You came," she said softly, and her face lit up with a beatific smile. Her eyes were drawn to the small tray in my hand and the smile grew even wider. Stepping back, she gestured at me to come in.

I stepped over the threshold and pulled the door closed behind me. The table was a jumbled mess of what must have been her dinner. An almost empty glass of wine, half a loaf of sour-dough bread, some cured ham, and a bottle of olive oil, along with an assortment of fruit, nuts, and candy bars in gaudy wrappers.

"This is what you had for dinner?" I asked. "Snickers and red wine?"

She smiled and wiped her paintbrushes on a stained cloth before putting them away. "I'm on holiday," she said with a grin. "What's for dessert?"

I cleared some space on the table and set the tray down. "*Schiacciata alla Fiorentina*," I said.

She came closer and I felt the tension rise.

"Mmm," she said. "Chocolate cake."

"No," I said. "It's *panforte*. Made from candied fruit, nuts and honey. Try it."

She pulled out a chair and I put one of the small plates in front of her. "*Buon appetit.*"

She licked her lips. "Looks yummy!" she exclaimed and took a spoonful. She tilted her head toward the ceiling and smiled as she tasted the dense sweet treat. Then her eyes sprung open and her eyebrows flew up as the complex spice mix hit her taste buds. "Oh!"

"It's no Snickers," I said drily, "but it's pretty good, no?"

She nodded slowly, taking another bite and exploring the flavors further. "Pretty damn good, yes."

I looked over at her paintings. At least half a dozen canvases were set out on every available surface, most of them with familiar motifs, clearly identifiable even though they weren't finished. "How's it going?" I asked.

She nodded, sucking the spoon as she followed my eyes. "Okay, I think. I should be done on time, as long as it doesn't keep raining."

"It has already stopped," I said. "Tomorrow, it will be sunny again." A couple of canvases stood on the floor behind the easel, facing the wall. "What are those?" I asked.

She waved one hand dismissively. "Nothing," she mumbled and took another bite of the cake before pushing the plate away. "This was really good. Thank you." She grabbed her wine glass and finished it off. Then she leaned back and smiled at me. "And thank you for coming. I mean it. I haven't spoken to a soul for three days. This was nice."

I felt bad. I hadn't come here for a conversation, and I had hoped that she would be as single-minded as I was about this. That we could just jump into bed and do that thing we had done so well, once more.

What was there to talk about, really? We were strangers, passing ships and all that.

And yet, I heard myself replying, "How come you're here alone?"

She gave me a crooked smile and glanced over at her paintings. "It's a long story." Then she looked straight at me. "I don't really feel like talking about it."

I looked back. "Then … what do you feel like?"

The crooked smile straightened. She leaned forward and placed one hand on my thigh. "It's late," she said quietly. "Let's just go to bed."

21

HEATHER

I HAD BEEN SO ABSORBED in my work that I hadn't noticed how late it was, but as soon as Marco showed up, I felt the long day in every part of my body. There was also a persistent sadness there that I didn't seem to be able to shake off.

It was good that he came. With his help, I would be able to get a good night's sleep.

The dessert was nice, even though it wasn't chocolate. But all I could think about were his soft lips and those skillful hands, and how they could make me feel.

Perhaps it was brash of me, but I didn't see any point in dancing around, pretending that this was something other than what it was. We weren't courting. Trying to get to know each other. Nothing like that.

We were just going to have sex. Mutually satisfying, casual sex. That was all there was too it.

Live and love with no regrets. Except that love didn't come into it.

Leaning forward, I placed one hand on his thigh and invited him to bed. The relief in his eyes was clear. Good. We were on the same wavelength.

He pushed the plates to one side, leaned over the table and kissed me. Gently at first and then more intensely. I got up off my chair and moved around the table to him, sliding into his lap. His hands moved slowly over my body as we kissed, searching for gaps in my clothing where he could get to my naked skin. After being apart for three days, my body responded immediately and violently to his touch, with something that almost felt like longing.

But that wasn't it. This was purely physical.

His fingers finally found their way in under my skirt and moved up along my naked thigh. They were so soft, yet strong, and I turned slightly to let them in between my thighs. Burrowing my fingers in his hair, I tilted his head up toward me to deepen our kiss and pressed my body against his firm chest. His fingers found the edge of my panties and slipped inside, and I sighed with anticipation. Oh, this was going to be good. Lifting my bottom just half an inch gave him just enough room to move where I needed it the most. Leaning forward a little placed more pressure on my clit and I felt my panties dampen. I slowly moved my hips back and forth in a barely noticeable movement that still managed to create a magnificent sensation in just the right spot.

I moaned against his lips and he responded by increasing the speed and pressure. This was going to be over fast. Well, I didn't mind that. We could always go again.

We had all night.

I pressed my breasts against his chest, feeling my tender nipples rubbing against the fabric. There was altogether too much fabric here. His stiff chef's jacket, my dress and bra.

Layers upon layers upon layers. So frustrating!

I struggled with the buttons on his jacket and managed to get them undone. Then I pulled the shoulder straps of my dress down and unhooked the bra. Tossing it over my shoulder, I pressed my naked breasts against his bare chest. It was hot and lean and hard, and I was filled with an intense longing for something that I couldn't quite name.

Marco's fingers rubbed me hard and fast, but his face looked completely calm as he broke away from our kiss to feast his eyes on my naked torso. Looking back up at my face, he slowly leaned forward and kissed the tip of one nipple with a featherlight peck that sent a lightning bolt straight into my core. Even before a moan made it across my lips, he had sucked that nipple deep into his mouth, and he started moving his tongue back and forth across it at the same time. My moan rose into a scream as I felt my inner muscles contract around his fingers.

He let go of my nipple and pulled me into a tight embrace. "That's right," he mumbled next to my ear, barely loud enough for me to make out his words. "That's good."

My whole body trembled and I couldn't reply. I just pulled him closer and whimpered helplessly.

Before I had managed to pull myself together, he had stood up, with me in his arms, and carried me into the bedroom, where he placed me gently on the bed.

I lay there, completely spent and obliterated by the orgasm, and couldn't do anything other than watch him slowly take his clothes off, standing next to the bed looking down at me. There was no hint of sadness in his beautiful eyes now, I noted. For this moment, at least, I had managed to vanquish his demons.

Once naked, he moved onto the bed on all fours, and I spread my legs wide, welcoming him. He stood over me, looking down at me with an intent stare in his eyes. He slowly lowered his head enough to kiss me, without touching me anywhere else. Once he had broken free from my lips, he moved slowly downward, placing scattered kisses here and there, on my neck, my breasts, my stomach, and then finally on the spot where my thighs met.

I whimpered as his tongue found my clit and tickled it back to life. It was too soon, I wanted to protest, but it wasn't, really. My body might have been knocked out, but it still wanted more. And more it got.

Marco buried his face in my folds, plunging his tongue deep inside and then following it with his strong fingers that knew all the right places. Sucking gently but rhythmically on my clit he coaxed ever louder whimpers from me until I once more screamed out loud. The bare walls echoed my screams back at me. At this stage I didn't care who heard me.

All I cared about was in this room, in this bed.

After the second orgasm, I felt broken, but in a good way. As Marco rose up between my legs and came toward me, I saw that he was fully erect. Part of me thought that I wouldn't be able to take it, but at this moment, I didn't even doubt that he would make it good, somehow.

I wanted to grab on to him, cling to him,

climb on top and ride him into the sunset, but was too wiped out from the strong sensations to do anything other than just lay there. Marco placed his swollen tip right by my entrance and slowly inched it in, little by little. The whole time he was looking me straight in the eye, searching for signs that I wanted him to stop, perhaps, because it must have been obvious that I wasn't capable of formulating any kind of objection.

But what was there to object to? I was getting the ride of my life.

Once he had pushed himself in to the hilt, he stopped and just lay there, filling me up. I wanted to say something, but what was there to say other than 'Don't stop!', and somehow, I knew that he didn't have any plans to.

I was going to remember this night for the rest of my life, that was for sure.

He waited for me, waited for what felt like an eternity, completely still, buried deep inside of me, until I had finally regained enough strength to begin to move again.

I lifted one hand and placed it against his cheek, rough with stubble after a long day. Looking him straight in the eye, I nodded.

He took his time, slowly picking up the pace until he was pumping hard against my swollen pussy. I felt raw and naked in a way I had never done before, not with anyone, but in a good way. It felt true. Honest.

And I had never felt this close to anyone, ever.

He came, and collapsed on top of me. I wrapped my arms around him, hoping that this feeling wouldn't be too hard to shake, once I'd left here.

After all. This was only a summer fling.

2 2

MARCO

COMING TOGETHER after three days apart was intense, but it was also exactly the release I'd been craving. She was so in tune with my needs; I could barely believe it. That a stranger could be everything that I wanted, everything that I hungered for …

It didn't feel quite right, but if this was what wrong felt like, then I'd rather be wrong, honestly.

She gave and I took, over and over, and in the end, I fell asleep in her arms.

I HADN'T MEANT to stay the night, but when I

woke up, the sun was streaming in through the window above the desk. Heather was already awake, lying on my outstretched arm, watching me with a sweet smile on her lips.

"Good morning," she said softly.

Her fingers were tracing invisible patterns up and down my chest, and one of her thighs was slung across my legs, right below my cock. It seems that part of me had already been up a while.

"Morning," I croaked.

Her fingers danced further down, circling my belly button in slow, languid movements, before continuing down to my groin. She grasped the semi-erect shaft with a gentle but determined hand, glancing up at me to judge my reaction.

"Sleep well?" she asked, completely casual, as if we'd met on the street.

I had, I realized. No dreams that I could remember, and even though it must have been way past midnight when we finally went to sleep, I felt rested in a way I hadn't for a long time.

I felt good.

The fact that my relaxed and comfortable

state made me feel bad said a lot about my state of mind. I did my best to push the guilt and shame to the side. There would be plenty of time to wallow in that later, once Heather had left.

When I didn't reply, her grip tightened. "Fine," I groaned. "I slept … fine."

She pouted. "Just 'fine'? I slept great. Like a log. Can't remember the last time I slept so good." The entire time she was talking, she was moving her hand up and down with a firm and determined stroke. I felt myself waking up in more ways than one. I leaned my head back and closed my eyes, letting all the blood in my body flow to where it was needed the most right now. I tried shifting her on top of me, but instead, she sat up next to me, ruffling her hair with her free hand and looking down at my now completely erect cock with an excited smile.

"I let you get the upper hand last night," she said. "This morning, it's my turn."

I stared at her as she leaned forward and wrapped her lips around my swollen tip, sucking it deep into her mouth. I felt the vacuum deep in my core and groaned out loud. Her fingers moved around my balls and the base of my shaft with impressive skill, and I tried not to think about all the cocks she must have sucked to learn that. It didn't matter. Why be jealous when I got to enjoy the fruits of her experience?

I had expected her to stop sucking and instead to straddle me for a ride, but she kept going, with both enthusiasm and intensity beyond anything I'd ever experienced. I reached for her, but she pushed my hand away, not letting me interrupt her.

In the end, there was nothing I could do except lay back and let it happen. The tension that was building was exquisite on the verge of torture, and it felt as if she was sucking the life straight out of me.

Well, with the way my life had been over the past ten years, she was welcome to it.

When I came, I could barely mumble a warning to her, but she didn't stop. Instead, she kept up the sucking until I'd emptied myself completely. Then she slowly released me and looked up at me with a pleased smile.

"Now, we're even," she said. She sat up, looking at the window. "I need to get going. I have so much work left to do on those paintings for your mother."

And just like that, she was gone. I lay there, completely limp and helpless, as she jumped off the bed and disappeared into the bathroom. The shower turned on, and I suffered greatly, picturing her luscious body with the water streaming down it, without being able to go to her, and give her something in return for what she'd just given me.

I lay there, listening to her getting ready, and had just managed to sit up on the edge of the bed when she reappeared, fully dressed and in the midst of securing her long, dark hair in a bun.

She smiled at me. "Will I see you tonight?"

As if I had a choice. As if I could have said no. "Yes. After dinner."

She came over to me, leaned forward, giving me an exhilarating view of her cleavage, and kissed me deeply. "Looking forward to it," she said, once she had broken free. And then she disappeared out into the other room.

I found my clothes scattered around the

room and pulled them on. When I came out into the other room, she was gone. The door outside was open, and after a minute or so, she reappeared. Grabbing some more paint supplies, she headed for the door again. "The sun is high in the sky," she said over her shoulder. "I have so much to catch up on."

When I came out into the garden, she had already set up her easel and was rummaging through her large wooden box for paints. She didn't look up as I walked past, and that was supposed to be a relief, except it wasn't.

It is great that she isn't clingy, I told myself. This is perfect. Exactly what I needed. It's just about the sex, and once that's done, she's all about her art, and I'm all about …

Yes. What?

What did I have that absorbed me the way that her art did her? I looked up at the *monasterio*'s withered brick walls. This place? My cooking?

For ten years, I had told myself that this was my life, but the sad truth of the matter was that I wouldn't be able to keep this up much longer. There was no way to make this business profitable. The bills had piled up for so long, and by the end of the year, I might have to throw in the towel. Tell my mother that she would have to sell the place.

I'd be out of a job and lose my apartment at the same time.

Then, what would I do?

Casting one last look on the beautiful woman who was absorbed by her painting, I continued inside and went up to my apartment. I showered, changed and made myself a cup of espresso. Then I walked over to the window and looked down.

I couldn't imagine what my life would look like if I didn't live here, if I didn't work here. But perhaps that was why I had let Heather come this close. I needed something —some*one*—to jolt me out of my rut.

So that I would be able to move on, both emotionally and physically.

HEATHER

ON MY LAST day at the *monasterio*, I woke up early again. Marco was sound asleep next to me, face down, his broad shoulders a fascinating landscape of lines and shadows.

Four nights we'd had together, and it had been the most amazing experience of my life. I could never have imagined that I'd be able to get this close to a stranger, but there was a real connection here; there was no denying that. I knew next to nothing about him, and he knew nothing about me, and it was fine, just the way it was.

Or so I kept telling myself.

I was leaving here today. Leaving him.

And watching him sleep next to me on

sheets we had rumpled beyond belief over the past few nights, that idea suddenly didn't seem that appealing.

I had to go. I had plans. Tickets to move on from Florence to Rome, and then to Naples in another two weeks before I went to Sicily. There was a whole long and detailed itinerary, but at the moment I couldn't remember a single item on it. There had been so many things I had wanted to see before I came here. So many places to visit. So much to explore.

And now, I didn't want to leave this room.

Frowning, I pushed the sheets to one side and slid out of bed, careful not to wake Marco. Pulling on the bathrobe I went into the other room. My paintings were lined up; all finished except the varnish. I was pleased with the results, even the ones that I had made as backups in case *signora* Balducci didn't like any of my first five. I walked along the row of canvases, checking for flaws, mistakes, anything I had overlooked. There was no denying that I had been a bit distracted over the past few days, and I hadn't gotten as much sleep as I might have needed, but it didn't show in my work. The intense nights with Marco had energized me, and I had put all that energy into my art. *Signora* Balducci would be pleased with the finished paintings; I was sure of that.

I stood for a long time watching the first painting, the one with the view over the valley, thinking. When I heard Marco stirring in the bedroom, I went and slipped a pod in the coffee maker.

He appeared in the doorway, his hair tousled, rubbing the sleep from his eyes. Bare-chested and with his checkered chef's trousers hanging low on his hips, he made my mouth water.

"Good morning, sunshine!" I said, replacing the cup in the coffee machine and slipping another pod in. "I've had an idea that I wanted to run by you." I handed him the first cup of coffee and he took it, sipping the hot liquid while he watched me warily above the rim.

Then he slowly lowered the cup. "What kind of idea?"

I nodded toward the paintings. "I'd like to

arrange an art retreat here. Maybe next summer?"

He didn't reply, so I walked over to the paintings, gesturing toward them. "This place is simply made for artists. Everywhere you turn, there's a motif worthy of portraying. And the weather's lovely, most of the time. People will pay good money to come and stay in a place like this, eat your yummy cooking and paint this amazing scenery." I turned toward him. "Don't you think?"

He frowned but didn't say anything.

"Oh," I said, disheartened. "You already have a retreat? Of course you do. I should have figured." I went back to the coffee maker and got the other cup. "Forget I said anything." I tried to take a sip of the coffee, but it was too hot. Holding the cup to my lips, I blew on the liquid to cool it.

"No," he said. "We've never had anything like that here. It's not that."

I perked up a little. "What then?"

He took another sip of coffee and then put the cup down on the kitchen table. "Next summer … Someone else will be running the place." He glanced up at me. "I can give them your contact info if you like. But I can't make any promises, because I won't be here."

I stared at him. It was strange, but I couldn't imagine this place without him. "Where are you going?"

He shook his head. "I don't know."

I frowned. "Then … why are you leaving?" This didn't make any sense.

He glanced toward the door, clearly uncomfortable. "It's not that I don't want to stay," he said. "It's just that a place like this, the upkeep is enormous, and since we have so few guests …" He shrugged. "It's just not working out. We're going to have to sell it. Probably sometime within the next six months or so."

I walked over to the table and leaned my butt against it. "I don't understand. I thought that you had few guests by choice. That you wanted to keep it exclusive."

He shook his head. "No, no, not at all. It's just … there are so many places like this, all over Italy—"

I almost choked on my coffee. "Are you kidding me? I can't imagine that there is a single place quite like this in the world. If people aren't lining up to stay here, it must be because they have no idea that this place exists. What does your marketing plan look like?"

He looked confused. "Marketing plan?"

I nodded. "Yes. What kinds of promotions do you do?"

He frowned. "We have a website, for bookings," he said vaguely. "And Elana set up a Facebook page, I think."

I raised my eyebrows. "You *think*? What about your mother? This was her place, you said. What does she do?"

He shook his head. "She's never been involved. She bought this place with the money my father left her, thinking that it would be an investment, but it hasn't paid off."

I looked at him, feeling myself being pulled in but resisting it. I was leaving here today, and by the sound of it, I wasn't ever coming back. Even if I did, he might not be here.

Glancing over my shoulder at my paintings, I realized that I might not want to come back here to paint if he wasn't here.

Frowning, I took another sip of the hot

coffee. I should go and take a shower. I should pack. I should prepare to leave.

But looking at Marco, standing there looking lost and sad, my heart reached out to him and pulled me with it.

"There's so much you could do," I said. "If you wanted to make this business profitable. That grand hall, for instance, where I worked the other day when it was raining? You should hold weddings there, and grand parties. Birthdays, anniversaries, that sort of thing. That would bring in lots of money, and you already have the staff and the kitchen, and … well, you. They would come here for your cooking."

He looked embarrassed, but I could tell that he knew that what I was saying was true.

"With a proper marketing campaign, you could fill every room in the building, all season, no problem. Run some ads on social media, of course, but you should also find the best travel shows and magazines and get them to feature you. Perhaps offer some influencers a free weekend here and see what happens." I took a deep breath. "And let me hold art retreats here. I promise you. People will come from all over the world and pay good money to stay here."

He rubbed a hand over his face. "I don't know," he said and looked pained. "I haven't a clue about how to do any of those things. I'm just a cook."

I pouted. "'*Just* a cook'? You should see about getting one of those Michelin guys to come for dinner one night. They'll slap a bunch of stars on your ass, and then you'll be turning dinner guests away all year round."

He just stared at me. Then he shook his head. "I don't know …" he said again. "Maybe it could have been possible to turn it all around, at some point but … things like this take time, and I just don't have that. The business is in the red and has been for too long. The bank isn't going to lend me any more money. So, I'm sorry. You'll have to find someplace else to hold your painting retreat."

Seeing his resigned face, I felt something shift inside me. I took a deep breath, put the coffee cup down on the table and walked over to the easel. Walking around behind it, I looked down at the canvas that stood on the floor there, out of sight, turned toward the wall.

Marco's half-turned away profile, the one from my dream. The charcoal drawing I had made after our first night together. I picked it up, staring at it. Then I looked over at him.

I hadn't meant for this to happen. It was just supposed to be a brief summer fling. But there was no point in pretending that I didn't care about what happened to this place. That I didn't care about what happened to Marco.

Because I did. I cared about Marco very much.

Too much, perhaps?

Because I knew that he didn't feel the same way about me. I knew that this had only been about the sex for him. I don't know what had brought on the sadness that was almost always present in his eyes, but I knew that he'd never want to tell me about it. We didn't have that kind of relationship.

Hell, we didn't have a relationship, at all.

The question was, if he didn't want me to be a part of his life after today, would he want to accept my help, if it meant that he could keep the *monasterio*?

MARCO

ALL THE THINGS she was talking about, it was all so obvious now that she had pointed it out to me. I couldn't believe that I hadn't thought about any of it myself before now. Not that I had the slightest idea about social media ads or what influencers were, but I was sure that I could have figured it out. If I'd only had the time.

By now, it was too late to turn this disaster around. Bar a miracle, we would have to sell the *monasterio* before the end of the year, and my mother would probably not even get back what she had paid for it.

I would be homeless and unemployed,

and I would have wasted my father's inheritance.

Sighing, I rubbed my neck and looked over at Heather. She was standing in the shadows across the room, looking at a painting. She looked sad. A bit puzzled. Then she glanced up at me, and I saw a glint in her eye. As if she was about to start crying.

But then she pulled herself up and put the painting back on the floor, and she came toward me, tucking the bathrobe tighter around her. She was undressed, unshowered, with no makeup and her hair tangled and tousled after an intense night with me, and she was the most beautiful woman I had ever seen.

She was a stranger. A passing stranger that I had spent some of the greatest nights of my life with. In a few short hours she would leave here, and I would never know anything about her.

It was for the best; I knew that. I had nothing to offer a woman like her. I was way too old, and I had no proper home and would soon be out of a job. She was an amazing artist, and she had so much to offer some lucky young man.

I just hoped that she would find someone who was good enough for her. After what she had given me this week, it seemed important to me that she would be happy.

But the idea of her with another man chafed and bothered me in a way I didn't like.

"These paintings over here," she said, gesturing to five canvases that stood along the back wall, "are the ones I made for your mother."

I looked at them. They were all stunning. "She'll be very pleased with them, I'm sure. I don't know how we'll be able to pay you for them, but I'll see to it that you get the money she promised you."

She looked at the paintings. "But they won't be enough," she said. "Prints and post-cards aren't going to turn this place around."

"No," I said. "It's too little, too late."

She glanced over at me. "What you need is an influx of capital," she said. "To tide you over until you've had time to implement all the changes this place needs to turn a profit."

I grimaced. "Like I said, the bank isn't going to loan us any more money."

She bit her lip. "I could lend it to you."

I stared at her, thinking that I must have heard her wrong. "Excuse me?"

"I could lend you the money," she said, fingering the belt on her bathrobe instead of looking at me. "I could cancel my plans to go to Rome, and stay here and we could make a business plan and a marketing plan and—"

"No!" I said abruptly. I shook my head and lowered my voice. "No, you mustn't change your plans. And I could never take your money. That would be completely out of the question."

She looked embarrassed. "I'm sorry," she said. "That was too forward of me, I know."

"It's not that," I said. But I couldn't have said what it was if I had all day and a pile of dictionaries to my disposal.

It wasn't even the fact that she'd offered me money that had upset me so. It was that she had offered to stay.

Two more weeks of *signorina* Heather, and there was no telling what would happen.

But one thing was for sure.

I wouldn't be able to pretend like what we had was just about the sex.

25

HEATHER

I EXCUSED myself and went to take a shower, but no amount of water could wash away the embarrassment of what had just happened. Why had I said that? And why had I said it in that way, as if I … What?

As if I was some corporate angel who knew anything about making a business profitable and had millions at my disposal.

Rubbing my face, I groaned. Who was I trying to kid? I was just a girl who loved to paint.

And if that girl happened to have some money that her grandfather had left her, then that didn't mean that it was a good idea to invest it in some scheme on the other side of the world, just because of some guy.

I tried to tell myself that it wasn't about Marco, but not very convincing.

Of course it was about Marco.

Leaning against the cool tiles, I bit my lip and did my best to keep the tears from flowing over. Stupid, stupid Heather. This was all supposed to be over soon, and now I would leave here feeling all awkward. Knowing that I had embarrassed Marco and …

Rome, I thought. Focus on Rome. All the things you wanted to see there. It was going to be amazing. I couldn't wait to paint the Colosseum. The ruins.

It was going to be awesome.

But rinsing the shampoo from my hair, I couldn't keep the tears back anymore.

It was going to be awful.

Because Marco wasn't going to be there.

<hr>

I WAS ALL PACKED. *Signora* Balducci's paintings had been varnished and were hanging in the grand hall waiting for her return and final approval. It had felt a bit presumptuous of me to hang my work in the same space as that beautiful old mural, but even I had to admit that my paintings had looked pretty good in the space. The receptionist, Elana, had been very helpful and she had complimented my work, but I hadn't been able to appreciate it. She must have thought me very distant. But in fact, I had been more present than I had ever been in my life.

Walking through the *monasterio* on my way back to the garden suite, I couldn't help but feel a pang of loss as I looked around me. There was so much here that I hadn't even had time to explore. So much more to do. So many more paintings I could have made.

So many more nights I could have spent with Marco.

I didn't know if I could have helped him turn this place around and make it into a profitable business. I had never done anything like that.

But I would have liked to try, at least.

It could have been amazing.

And then what, a quiet voice at the back of

my mind said. *If you had been able to save the* monasterio, *then what?*

I stopped on the threshold and looked out over the immaculate garden, breathing in the scents of the rosemary bushes and the lemon trees.

Then we would have lived here together, happily ever after, a silly voice replied from some dark crevasse at the back of my mind.

Lived and loved.

Pushing the silly fantasies to the side, I stepped down onto the gravel path and walked back to the garden suite to collect my luggage.

It was a lovely fantasy, but not one that I could ever believe in, unfortunately.

Because as much as I knew that Marco was the one, I also knew that he didn't love me.

26

MARCO

I STOOD AT THE WINDOW, looking down at the garden when Heather appeared, walking along the path toward the garden suite. She would be leaving soon. I knew that. I had arranged for Sergio to drive her back to Firenze.

Perhaps I should have taken her myself, but I didn't have the time. There was so much I needed to prep before the dinner service. Or at least, that's what I had been telling myself.

Leaning against the window frame, I stared at her as she disappeared in the shadows on the other side of the garden.

What a woman. So beautiful. And so talented. So … alive.

She had certainly made me feel alive this week. No small feat.

And apparently, she could also help me turn this place into a profitable business.

I shook my head and grimaced. It was all too much. It was like the universe was taunting me. Look at this amazing woman. Look at all she has to offer you.

Heather was everything I never knew I wanted.

And she had offered to stay here for another two weeks. She had offered me money. After giving me everything night after night, she was now offering me a way out of bankruptcy, out of humiliation. Out of loneliness.

It was too good to be true. And if there was one thing I knew, it was that good things didn't come to a man like me. I'd had something good in my life once, and it had been taken from me.

What if I let Heather stay? What if I let myself love her … and then lost her?

It would kill me; I knew it would.

I would never be able to survive another loss like that.

It was much easier to just be alone. I knew where I stood with the loneliness. I knew I could bear it. I had done for the last ten years.

But would I be able to go back to that meager existence after these last few days with Heather? That was the question.

I pushed myself away from the window and turned around. My apartment looked unusually bare and dull, and I couldn't understand why that was. Heather had never been up here. She didn't even know that I lived here. She didn't know anything about me.

And I didn't know the first thing about her.

Her leaving was the best thing for both of us. In time, we would get over this. She would probably forget all about me as soon as she arrived in Rome.

Glancing at the clock on the microwave, I felt something sharp in my chest. Five more minutes or so. Then she would be gone.

I should go down and say goodbye. It was the least I could do.

I tried. I really did. But in the end, I only made it halfway down the narrow stairs from my apartment. Then I sank down onto a step in the darkness and just sat there, staring blindly into space.

There was no future for us; I knew that. And there was no future for the *monasterio*. It was just so hard to keep moving forward when there was nothing to work towards. Nothing to hope for.

All I had was what I had lost. First Giulietta. And now Heather. And I knew that what Heather and I had didn't compare to my marriage, but I couldn't help thinking about what we might have had. What might have been.

If I had been the kind of man that could have asked her to stay.

Burying my face in my hands, I gritted my teeth and pictured Heather getting into the car out front, right at this very minute. Sergio holding the door for her. She probably looked up at the grand brick façade, memorizing it for a future painting.

And then she slipped into the back seat and was driven down the road, away from me.

Something tore inside my chest and I gasped for air, leaning back against the steps.

So stupid of me to think that I could have a little fling. That it would be purely physical.

And that I would be able to just go on with my life after she had left.

How would I ever—

The door at the bottom of the steps opened, and a shaft of light invaded the cramped, dark space. Even backlit, I immediately recognized the silhouette.

"Heather," I breathed.

She leaned against the door frame, looking up at me, peering into the darkness. "Elana told me where to find you," she said. Her voice sounded different. Fragile, somehow. She turned her face slightly as she slipped inside the stairwell and pulled the door close, and I saw something glint on her soft cheek before we were both wrapped in darkness again. Had she been crying? Over me?

I felt more than saw her coming toward

me up the stairs. There was barely any light here. She sat down a couple of steps below me, squinting up at me in the dark.

"I thought you'd come to say goodbye," she said.

"I was on my way," I replied hoarsely. "And then ..."

She leaned back against the wall. "And then?"

I sighed. "I don't know ..." I mumbled.

She looked up at me. "I'm sorry if I offended you somehow," she said. "I didn't mean to. I just wanted to help."

Staring down at her, I swallowed. "You didn't do anything wrong. It was sweet of you to offer."

"But?"

I shook my head. "But ... there's just ... You don't know me. You don't know anything about me."

She nodded. "We're practically strangers."

"Exactly." I ran my fingers through my hair. "So, you see. It's better for everyone if you stick to your plan. Go to *Roma*. Have a great time. Make beautiful art."

She sniffled. "And what about you?"

I snorted. "What about me?"

She leaned forward. "What are you going to do?"

I shrugged. "I'll figure something out."

The idea of even getting up from these stairs and going on with my life without her suddenly felt completely unbearable. What would be the point of anything at all without her? But I couldn't let her know how I felt. It would only embarrass her. Or perhaps she would feel obligated to stay. I certainly didn't want that.

She had her whole life ahead of her. This had only been the first of many great adventures she would experience this summer.

"I could stay," she said quietly. "Just for another two weeks." She was silent for a while, but when I didn't reply, she continued. "It would give us enough time to … talk things through. Figure out where we stand."

I rubbed my face with one hand. Two more weeks with her would be hell, knowing that she would eventually leave. "You should go now," I said, and my voice sounded like that of a stranger.

She didn't move. "I don't want to," she

said eventually. "Not like this. This week has been amazing, and now … it feels as if I ruined it somehow, this morning, with what I said."

I shook my head. "You didn't do anything wrong, Heather."

"Then why were you gone when I got out of the shower?" she asked. "Why did you stay away all day? Why wouldn't you even come to say goodbye," she whispered. "I couldn't believe it when you didn't show up as I was leaving."

I looked down at her beautiful face, her large blue eyes gleaming in the dark. Reaching out one hand, I caressed her cheek. "It's not easy," I said, as honestly as I could, "to see you go."

She blinked rapidly. "Then why don't you want me to stay for two more weeks? We could have so much more time together."

I swallowed hard and told her the truth. "Because after two more weeks with you …" I said, "I don't think I'd ever get over you leaving."

27

HEATHER

MY HEART EXPLODED into a cloud of warmth that filled my entire chest. I had some difficulty believing what he was saying, but my body didn't care.

"Ask me to stay, Marco," I whispered, placing one hand on his leg. "Just say the word."

He shook his head violently, but I leaned forward, shifting up another step to get closer.

"Marco?" I said. "If you want me to stay, you only have to say so."

"Two weeks," he said. "It's not enough. It would only make it so much more difficult when you leave."

I slipped up between his legs, standing on my knees, looking him straight in the eyes. It was dark here in the stairwell, but I could see his eyes. The old pain was still there, but there was something else there as well. A new, fresh suffering. The idea that I had caused him even more pain was unbearable.

"Oh, Marco," I sighed and leaned forward to kiss him. I almost expected him to turn away, but he didn't. He kissed me back, slowly, tentatively, but not reluctantly.

Feeling his strong arms around me, I felt calmer than I had done all day. How had I ever believed that I could just walk away? Stupid, stupid Heather.

Caressing his cheek, I pulled back from the kiss and looked him in the eye. "I never meant to hurt you," I whispered. "I only ever wanted to make you feel good."

He leaned his forehead against mine. "It's not your fault," he said, and his voice sounded like gravel. "I was broken long before you got here."

Wrapping my arms around him, I pulled him close and held him tight. "Tell me," I whispered, right by his ear.

He held me so hard, I could barely breathe, and he was silent for so long that I didn't think he was going to reply, but in the end, he spoke.

"Her name was Giulietta," he said. "We were married. We were happy."

His words cut me like a knife, but I needed to know. "What happened?" I asked, trying to keep my voice neutral.

"A car accident," he said. "A drunk driver hit us one night coming home from dinner with some friends. He plowed straight into the passenger side of the car. I never saw him coming. One minute I was driving along, laughing at something Giulietta had said, and the next minute the whole world exploded. Glass fragments and airbags coming toward me from all directions. The impact was so loud, I couldn't hear anything for a long time, except for this ringing sound that seemed to cut through my skull."

I hugged him tighter and kissed his temple gently. There was nothing I could tell him that would make this better.

"I couldn't understand what had happened. It felt as if the sky had fallen or an earthquake or something. It was so much more violent than I'd ever have pictured a car accident. It took a minute or two before I understood what had happened. I sat there, surrounded by airbags that slowly deflated. I remember pushing them away from my face, looking around. Wiggling my toes and being relieved that I couldn't feel any specific pain. My body ached all over from the impact, but nothing seemed to be broken. I walked away from that wreck with barely a scratch. The miracle of airbags."

He leaned his head back, staring up at the ceiling. "We'd just gotten that car, after driving around in an old clunker for years. And I remember thinking as I pushed the airbags away from me, how lucky we were, because in our old car we would never have survived an accident like that. And then I looked over at Giulietta, and …"

His voice broke, and my heart, too. He took a deep breath and continued. "Her face was turned toward me, and her eyes were just … staring … And I knew right away that she was dead. The other car had demolished that whole side of the car. She had died instantly."

Holding him tight, I wept there in the dark. For Marco. For his wife. For all those years of pain.

Was it possible to ever get over that kind of loss? Would he ever be able to love again?

One thing was certain.

Two weeks wasn't going to be enough.

Two months later:

Elana and I stood outside the kitchen door, watching the wedding ceremony. It was only a medium-sized wedding party, but the bride had brought a gigantic wedding planner and a long list of requirements to the initial planning meeting, and I had known all along that it would be a challenge to please her. Thankfully, Elana had stepped up, and newly promoted to event coordinator she had fulfilled and surpassed all the bride's wishes for her big day. The wedding had been a roaring success, and I knew that word would spread. There had already been several bookings for parties, just from the bride's social media posts under the weeks leading up to the wedding, and I imagined that the pictures from today would fill the *monasterio's* calendar for the rest of the year, easily.

The place was transformed. Guests were flocking to the unique destination from all over. They came for the history, for the scenery, for the ambiance, and for the food. Marco had taken on more staff to manage the influx of business, and he was running the place as if he'd never done anything else in his life. Now that the tide had turned, he had broken out of his paralysis, and was constantly coming up with new ideas to market this gem. It was only a matter of time before he'd be turning a profit, and I expected my investment to pay off many times over.

The question was, what was I going to do now? The summer had come to an end without me having done any of the things on my travel itinerary. We had been so busy working here at the *monasterio* all summer that I had never gotten to see any other part of Italy. I didn't mind, not at all. It had been the best summer of my life.

But the date for my return flight was approaching, and I had a decision to make.

We had been too busy to talk about emotions or our relationship, but Marco seemed happy, and I certainly was. The only thing that worried me was the size of the commitment. I was still so young, and there was so much I hadn't done.

Was I really prepared to settle down in a foreign country, with a man twice my age? I knew that I loved Marco. But was that enough?

Looking at the young couple standing in front of the priest exchanging vows, I felt my eyes start to tear up. It was such a huge commitment, but they didn't seem afraid. Of course, they had known each other for years, and they had grown up in the same town. They had so much in common.

Marco and I came from different worlds.

Would love be enough to make up for all of our differences? Could we make this work with only our strong feelings for each other as a foundation?

The groom kissed the bride and the crowd cheered. They would all be moving into the grand hall for the reception, but I knew that the bride had something she wanted to do first. It wasn't an Italian custom, but I guess she had watched a few too many American rom coms. All the single women gathered together in front of the guests, and the bride turned her back on them. The women giggled and pushed and shoved to get in position.

With a determined throw, the bride hurled the pretty bouquet high up in the air and over her shoulder toward the assembled women. They all squealed and jumped to grab it.

In the huddle, there were a few that were set on catching the bouquet, but they all reached for it at the same time, and just as one hand was closing in on the flowers, another hand knocked it out of reach.

The intricate wedding bouquet sailed up in the air once more, and this time off to the side.

Straight toward me.

The gathered women howled in disappointment as they saw the flowers in my hands. I turned the bouquet over and stared at it. Elana elbowed me in the side and shouted something in Italian to the guests, who all started to move into the grand hall.

"The florist did a great job," I said to Elana, studying the arrangement. "Tell her for me, the next time you speak to her, okay? We will want to use her for the anniversary party next week as well."

Elana only laughed and walked away to get the reception started.

I stood there with the flowers as the garden emptied of wedding guests. The arrangement was beautiful, but it was what they symbolized that was getting me all emotional.

How had I ever thought that I would be able to go home at the end of the summer? What I had found here with Marco was so much more than a summer fling. As busy as I had been with getting the *monasterio* back in black, I had been painting all summer, and my work had never been better. I would have a show in the grand hall this winter, once the wedding season was over.

It wasn't the life I'd ever pictured for myself, and I still missed my friends so much it hurt.

But I couldn't imagine leaving this place. Not ever.

The door behind me opened. I glanced over my shoulder and saw Marco standing there.

"Heather," he said, his eyes glowing in that special way that they always did whenever he looked at me. Studying him, I saw that the pain and sadness was gone. He looked strong. Happy. Loving. "Do you have a minute?"

Clutching the bridal bouquet, I turned toward him, feeling my heart soar, as it always did in his presence. "Yes, Marco," I said. "I do."

THE END

Curious about what Laura's friends are up to this summer? Find out in their own novellas:

CATHERINE ALBA

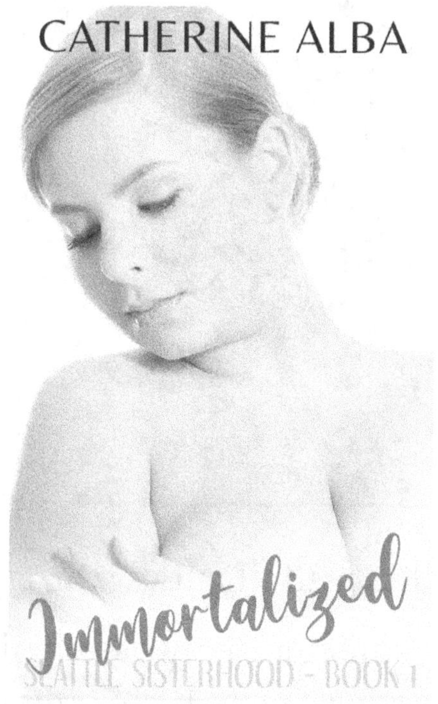

Immortalized - Felicity's story:

Staying behind in Seattle while my friends set off on great adventures was not the way I had planned to spend the summer after graduation, but here I was. Alone in a crappy apartment, working at the same old job that I'd had every summer since high school. This was going to be the worst summer ever!

Rescued - Laura's story:

Spending the summer in my parents' beach house figuring out what I want to do after graduation might have made me the envy of my friends, but the affluent Florida resort was no longer the paradise I'd known. I'd had a crush on the boy next door last summer, and it had ended badly. What a nightmare!

I could never have imagined that Mr. Lindstrom

would be the one who came to my rescue. Ironic that I would need to be saved from a lifeguard!

FELICITY

"THIS IS GOING to be the worst summer ever," I said, staring at the screen. My two best friends looked back at me, protesting in a chorus, each from their own little square on Zoom. Laura from her sunny room at her parents' vacation home on the Florida coast and Heather from her Airbnb in Florence, Italy. We'd never been this far apart. The three of us had met when we started junior high and stuck together through thick and thin since then.

It had been a while.

A lot of water under the bridge and all that. And perhaps a little more thick than thin, I thought, glancing down at my bulky bathrobe.

The fact that we were all on the plus size side of the spectrum had meant that I always felt that I fit in, even though I didn't look like the women I saw everywhere in ads and on social media. I was one part of a gorgeous, positive, and friendly trio of girls, and if my own confidence didn't always shine bright like a diamond, my wonderful friends had it to spare. They were everything to me.

And now, we'd be apart for the entire summer.

"It's going to be great," Laura said. "You'll have a blast, Felicity!"

Heather seemed to agree. Well, it was easy for them to say. They both had exciting plans for the summer after graduation. Laura had her parents' luxurious beach house in Florida all to herself and was spending the summer working on her tan, surrounded by buff lifeguards. Heather was traveling through Italy, painting and studying art, and would probably be meeting lots of exciting Italian men.

And me? I was stuck here in Seattle, working at the same coffee place where I'd been working for the last three summers.

My friends were off to see the world, and I was stuck here at home.

"I'm going to miss you guys," I said and tried not to sound *too* pathetic. I may have failed. "It's going to be so weird, not having you around."

Heather leaned forward toward the screen. "You know what, Felicity. It *is* weird. As much as I've been looking forward to this trip, I am a little bit scared of being out here, all alone." She smiled and I could see her eyes move from side to side as she looked at our faces on her screen. "But perhaps you should see it as an opportunity to try new things. Just because you're back home in Seattle, doesn't mean that everything has to be the way it's always been."

I shrugged. "Everything *is* going to be the way it's always been," I said. "I've been working at The Grind every summer since high school. The only thing that'll be different is that I won't have you guys around."

"Perhaps you should get a new job, then," Heather said.

I frowned. "Maybe."

I didn't like the idea. New things scared me. New places. New experiences. It wasn't my thing. The only reason I ever tried anything new was because my friends wanted to do it, and I tagged along, for their sake, not my own.

I liked things to stay the way they were.

I could hear my friends talking but didn't register what they said.

Get a new job? No. I liked working at The Grind. I knew where everything was, and it was usually a pretty chill gig. Nice people.

If I didn't have my friends around all summer, I certainly didn't want to lose my job friends as well.

But perhaps Heather was right.

Perhaps I needed to try *something* new this summer. Something different. Step outside my comfort zone. Just this once.

"Felicity?"

The sound of my name brought me back to the conversation. "Yes?"

It was Heather, in Italy. "Could you do me a huge favor?"

I perked up. "Of course. Anything."

"I just got an email from my professor. They're doing some remodeling at the art studios on campus, and if I don't collect my paintings from the graduation show before the end of next week, they might get damaged, or even thrown out. There are two of them. Do you think you could …?"

"Of course. I'll go and pick them up today." That would give me something to do. I didn't have a shift at The Grind until tomorrow morning.

"Thanks, Fee. You're a darling."

A lonely darling, I thought.

We all signed off, and I closed my laptop and just sat there for a while, looking around me. At the strange and unfamiliar room, with just the bed, a small table and a couple of chairs, bare walls and empty shelves. The stack of moving boxes I still hadn't unpacked. It felt so weird, being all alone for the first time in my life. I had more or less assumed that we'd all get a place together after graduation, after sharing a suite on campus for three years, and I hadn't really made any plans beyond going along with whatever my friends suggested.

But life had taken us all in different directions, and despite Heather and Laura's promises, I wasn't entirely sure that they'd be back in August, like they'd said. None of them had wanted to commit to a shared lease, so here I was, in the tiniest, cheapest, dullest apartment I'd been able to find. But was it just the temporary solution that I'd tried to picture it as, or was this the beginning of the rest of my life? What if they never came back? Then what would I do?

It would be two whole months, before I knew for sure. Two long, boring, and kind of depressing months. How was I ever going to get through this summer without my friends around?

And what would I do if they didn't come back?

The thought gave me chills.

I was nothing without Heather and Laura.

Getting a new job, trying new things. None of that was ever going to happen without my brave and fearless friends around.

I got up from the bed where I'd been sitting and walked over to my wardrobe. Even my clothes were dull and ordinary. I just didn't feel comfortable drawing attention to my body. Not like Heather, who was always a vision in flowy hippie skirts and shawls. The typical artist. Laura was a little more like me, in that she wore more muted colors and nothing too sexy or flashy. Well, she didn't need spectacular clothes to get everyone's attention. She was the beauty in our little group. Laura had the looks, Heather was the artist.

And me? What did I bring to the table?

I'd asked myself that question numerous times over the years and never come up with an answer. I was just Fee, the third friend.

Three was a crowd, wasn't it? But it had never felt that way with Heather and Laura. It had always been the three of us, and that had never been a problem. We'd all been so different. But the only thing special about me had always been that there was nothing special about me.

I reached for a T-shirt, but my hand stopped mid-air. Always a T-shirt and jeans, every day of the year. *Try new things,* I heard Heather's voice echo through my mind. *Everything doesn't have to be the way it's always been.*

My hand wandered along the railing in my closet, but everything there was the same. Subtle. Nondescript. Camouflage. A spark of color right at the back caught my eye. Oh, it was one of Heather's old dresses that she'd handed down to me last summer when she went up a size. It was beautiful, but I'd never worn it. It was too bright, too colorful, with a large and bold flower pattern on a white background. It clung to my body and had a big, twirly skirt. It was a beautiful dress. I just didn't have the personality to match. It had looked great on Heather, but I couldn't pull it off.

I took the dress off the hanger and stood in front of the mirror, holding it up in front of me. I'd told myself I was saving it for a special occasion. That this dress was too pretty for everyday wear. But if I ever went to a party, I'd never wear a dress like this. If I were going out to a place with a ton of people, I'd want clothes that I felt comfortable in. Clothes that made me blend in.

But this *was* a special occasion. It was the first day of my Summer of Solitude. I'd always had my friends here with me, for as long as I could remember. This summer was going to be such a drag. The worst summer ever.

Unless … Unless I found the courage to step outside of my comfort zone. To wear the pretty dress. *Try something different,* Heather's voice said.

So I pulled on her dress, grabbed my phone and car keys, and left the apartment before I lost my nerve.

BRENT

I HAD BEEN WORKING LATE last night. Every night this week. Working harder than I'd ever worked before to get this painting to where I wanted it to be. I had thought I'd been making progress, finally. But this morning, when I got to the studio and saw my work in the bright morning sun, I'd wanted to vomit.

Seeing my painting had made me feel sick. Physically sick. The flat colors. The nondescript lines. The … nothingness of it all. So many hours of work, and all I wanted to do was to throw it out and start over.

The image I wanted to capture was so clear in my mind, but I hadn't been able to transfer it onto the canvas.

The frustration would be the death of me. I could feel it grinding me down. Perhaps I had lost it. Perhaps my time as an artist was over.

Those who can, do. Those who can't, teach. My wife's spiteful voice echoed through my head. Was that true? And if so, was that the reason that I had taken this job? Had I known deep inside that I didn't have what it took to be an artist? Or was it the teaching job that had been wearing me down? Making me lose my focus on art. On beauty.

This place was so ugly. There was nothing here that sparked my creativity. Everything was just work and routines and schedules and classes and critiques. I only had a few hours now and then to work on my own paintings. And that wasn't enough. I needed to be able to really spend time with my art. Needed to nurture it. I needed a muse.

But there were no muses on campus. Only students that I was absolutely forbidden to lust after. That would get me fired faster than I could say 'fraternization'.

I sighed and walked over to the coffee machine, refilling my cup. At least it was the summer break now. I would only be teaching one summer course this year, so that should give me more time to work on my own art. On top of that, figure studies was a beginner's course, something I had taught so many times I didn't even need to prepare for the classes. All I'd had to do was hire the models. I had found a male model already, and I'd had a young woman lined up for the other position, but her mother had been taken ill, and she'd had to go home for the summer. I would have to find another female model before tomorrow night.

I sighed and sipped the coffee. Where was I going to find a woman who'd be willing to take off all of her clothes in front of strangers, on such short notice?

There was a knock on the door. I turned around. "Enter," I said.

The door opened. A young woman stood there, her hand on the door handle. "Excuse me," she said. "I'm here to collect a couple of paintings. From the graduation showing? I was told that they had been brought to this building when the exhibition closed."

I stared at her. She was beautiful. A vision of femininity, fertility, curves, and glory. She was wearing the most spectacular dress with bright, big flowers, and the fabric seemed to be molded to her magnificent body. Where she was standing, in the doorway, she was lit from behind in a way that made it look as if she was glowing. Radiant.

I slowly lowered my coffee cup, trying to remember how to string words together to form a sentence in reply. "I think they put them in the main atelier, down the hall," I said. "The door at the end."

"Oh," she said. "Thank you. Sorry if I disturbed you." She waved a little and closed the door again.

I just stood there, staring at the closed door, the image of her glowing figure imprinted on my retina. Oh, she had disturbed me, alright. On so many levels. I didn't know if I wanted to tear off that beautiful dress and ravage her amazing body, or if I wanted to put her on a podium and just paint her from every conceivable angle.

Something had awoken inside of me, something that I hadn't realized had been dormant for so very long. A passion. A hunger. A desire. The creative spark that had been missing from my art for so long.

The point of it all.

I couldn't let her leave.

Slamming the coffee cup down on the windowsill, I hurried toward the door. The corridor was empty. The door at the end was ajar. With brisk and determined steps, I closed the distance between us in just a couple of seconds.

She was the muse I had been pining for. She was *it*.

The atelier was empty. The next class wasn't until tomorrow evening. On the podium in the middle of the room stood a chaise-longue, draped in a silky fabric. Surrounding the podium, several easels, spaced out. And her. As I entered, heart pounding, she spun around.

"Oh," she said. And then she smiled.

That smile. It destroyed me. Broke me down. Tore away the cobwebs and the dreariness that had coated everything in my life for so long.

I had to force myself to get a grip. She was a student. Completely out of bounds. Not to mention the fact that I was married. And twice her age, easily.

But I had to make her mine, on some level.

"Did you find what you were looking for?" I asked and hoped that she couldn't tell that I was almost out of breath, just from looking at her. Being in the same room as her.

She was other-worldly. Unnaturally

beautiful. I'd never seen anything like it. I wanted to drop to my knees and worship her. Or at the very least, paint her. Sketch every line. Every curve. Imprint it on my brain, so that I'd never forget that I had once been in the presence of perfection. Pure and undiluted beauty.

I had never, ever felt this way before. And I still considered myself something of a ladies' man. Sure, I was married, and I mostly stayed inside the boundaries of that marriage, even though I was pretty sure that my wife didn't. But I had never stopped looking. Appreciating. Studying.

I could try and brush it off as an art thing. That I just appreciated the human form. But I couldn't care less about most human forms.

It was *this one* that I had been searching for all my life.

"No," she said, and I had to think really hard before I realized what she was talking about.

"They probably put the paintings in the supply room," I said, walking over to the door across the room. It was locked, and I pulled out my keys and unlocked it. A couple of dozen paintings stood on the floor leaning against the wall at the back, each of them enveloped in a thick layer of bubble wrap. On every artwork was a strip of masking tape with a name in sharpie. "I didn't catch your name," I said, trying hard not to stare at her. It was difficult. I didn't ever want to look away.

She seemed to hesitate. Then she said, "Heather. Heather Branson."

I looked at the paintings, scanning the names. "Here." I pulled out two small paintings and handed them over.

"Thank you," she said. Another smile. Then she turned and walked through the studio toward the door. The dress danced around her bare legs as she moved. It was hypnotizing.

I couldn't let her leave. What if I never saw her again? The idea made my chest hurt. Not to mention my groin.

If I asked her to sit for me, she'd probably balk at the idea. Think me a pervert or something. But perhaps …

"Heather?" I said.

She glanced over her shoulder at me.

"Are you staying in town this summer?"

She looked hesitant. Perhaps even a little sad. Then she nodded.

"One of our models had do drop out." I jerked my head toward the podium. "Have you ever sat?"

Her eyes widened. Strange. She must have been asked a hundred times before. Every art student on campus must have wanted to draw her, sketch her, paint her, sculpt her.

Make love to her until dawn.

I pushed the idea out of my mind. This was *not* about sex. She was a student and off-limits. And I was a married man. An *old*, married man.

But she made me want to paint in a way I hadn't experienced in a long time. She made me want to create beautiful works of art.

And I couldn't let her leave. I just had to paint her.

"Please," I said. "You would be doing me a huge favor. It doesn't pay much, but it's only one night a week."

She glanced at the podium. Swallowed. The hesitation was apparent. I was sure that she was going to say no. But then she said, "Alright."

The relief almost brought me to my knees. She would do it. She would sit for my life drawing class. I would be able to study her for two hours every Monday night for eight weeks. After that, I would be able to paint her from memory.

After that, I would never be able to forget her.

CONTINUE READING Felicity and Brent's story in Immortalized.